A
Killing
in the
Real
World

A Killing in the Real World

A Novel

Christopher A. Bohjalian

St. Martin's Press
New York

A KILLING IN THE REAL WORLD. Copyright © 1988 by Christopher A. Bohjalian. All rights reserved. Printed in the United States of America. No part of this book may be used or reproduced in any manner whatsoever without written permission except in the case of brief quotations embodied in critical articles or reviews. For information, address St. Martin's Press, 175 Fifth Avenue, New York, N.Y. 10010.

Editor: Jared Kieling

Design by Judith Stagnitto.

Library of Congress Cataloging-in-Publication Data

Bohjalian, Christopher A.
    A killing in the real world / by Christopher A.
Bohjalian.
        p. cm.
     ISBN 0-312-01781-2
     I. Title.
PS2552.0495K5 1988   87-38252
813'.54—dc 19

First Edition

10 9 8 7 6 5 4 3 2 1

for Victoria

I

Wednesday

1

Lisa's Dream

Lisa Stone slept curled in a ball, a grown woman rolled on her side into a croissant, and dreamt. She dreamt she was atop the steeple of the Edwards Church in Winston, the tallest point in the small Massachusetts town. She was standing back on her heels with one arm wrapped around the steeple's apex, the wind trying to blow open her winter coat. To her left, the town spread out below her in neat little squares that eventually faded into the Berkshires. To her right was Crosby College, an eclectic series of cozy white houses and gothic spires—one of the few remaining women's colleges of real merit. She could not pinpoint her old dormitory because it was blocked by a series of ivy-covered administration buildings.

She huddled closer to the tip of the church and stared at the clock tower on College Hall, essentially the entrance to Crosby College. The tower was about one hundred yards away, a structure almost—but not quite—as tall as the Edwards steeple. She was not sure how long she had been clinging to the steeple when she first saw them. Her old roommates and housemates. One by one she watched them line up on the ledge of the tower, all of them dressed in their white Founder's Day graduation gowns, all of them again twenty-one. Led by Penny Noble, they threw themselves off the ledge, taking the time to fall the seventy-five feet to the ground that one only gets in a dream. But despite their eerie, gentle descent, they hit the pavement with an all too real brutality. Christine Yarbrough. Melanie Braverman. Kate Hemmick. Their bodies lay twisted on the ground unnaturally, great splotches of blood growing across their gowns.

"Stop it!" she screamed to the women remaining on the ledge, "Stop!" But the wind choked off her voice before it carried even across the street.

II

Thursday

2

"Noble Woman Dies with Filth"

"Well, where did she meet him?" Melanie Braverman asked over the telephone. "It sure wasn't at a Junior League lunch."

"No, sure wasn't," Lisa Stone said, trying to envision him—the man New York's smarmiest tabloid, the *Post*, called a pimp and pornographer—eating watercress sandwiches in a room full of kilts. It almost made her smile—but not quite.

"What about her family? God, Lisa, they must be completely blown away. Completely wasted," Melanie continued, her mind scooting among questions like a sand crab.

"I doubt they're 'wasted,' Melanie," Lisa answered, chastening her friend in Boston. "They're upset. They're in shock. They're crying. But they're not wasted."

"It's just an expression," Melanie said, her voice trailing off into a sniffle. "You know I'm as upset about this as you are."

"Then don't talk about it like a teenager! Penny's dead! You can't use words like 'wasted' or 'blown away' now." It had always astounded Lisa that no matter what she and Melanie were talking about, Melanie could make the subject sound adolescent. That was fine when they met ten years ago, when they were seventeen; but now at twenty-seven, it tended to irritate Lisa.

"I'm sorry, Lisa, but it amazes me. I don't think I've ever known anyone before who was shot. And I know I've never lived with anyone who was."

"Oh, don't apologize," Lisa said, recovering slightly. "I'm probably oversensitive. After all, I've never known anyone before who made the front page of the *New York Post*."

"Could you read me the articles? If it's too painful, don't. I can see them when I get to New York."

Cradling the phone between her shoulder and her ear, Lisa stared at the headline she had read and reread all morning. Each time she saw it, she had received the same sickening jolt. "Noble Woman Dies with Filth." She ran her fingers over each two-inch letter, hoping that when she reached to touch them, she would find they were not actually there.

"No, I'll read them," Lisa said tiredly. "But it's ghoulish. I'm ghoulish. For a change I know the raped nun or the burned-up baby on the front page, and I don't like the feeling. Not one bit." She leaned forward over her desk, allowing her head to rest on one hand while holding the phone with the other. "Which one do you want to hear first? The *New York Post*? The *Daily News*? Or the *Times*?"

"It's in all three?"

"Sure is."

"God, I thought only the *Post* had made a big deal of it."

"No," Lisa said, noticing the black smudges on her hands for the first time that morning. "It's in them all."

"I don't see it anywhere in the *Boston Globe*," Melanie said as she flipped through that paper, sounding almost as if she thought Boston had been slighted somehow.

"What did you expect? It was a New York murder. I

don't get to read about every Boston massacre in the New York papers."

"But this is different," Melanie continued, her voice cracking. "Penny went to Crosby College."

"She went to Crosby six years ago," Lisa said softly, trying to sooth Melanie with what little composure she had left.

"But it was still Crosby," Melanie said with sad irony. "I would think a murdered Crosby alum is big news."

"Please, Melanie. Choose your poison. I can't stand having these on my desk much longer."

"Start with the *Post*, I guess. Let's get the worst over with first."

"Okay," Lisa said, staring at the dark round eyes in the photograph on the front page. Those were Penny Noble's eyes, there was no mistaking them. They sparkled. Even in black and white they sparkled, even as part of a grainy tabloid photograph blown up to twice its size. And that was Penny's smile, the camera somehow noting not only that it was slightly lopsided, but that it had a quiver to it, an air of vulnerability.

"The headline is, 'Noble Woman Dies with Filth.' The letters are a good two inches long. The bottom corner is her picture."

"Do you recognize the shot?"

"Sure do. It's her engagement photo from The *New York Times*. But they're in a lot closer than Bachrach ever intended."

"Is it pretty?"

"Is she pretty? Well, yes. Of course. But the reproduction stinks. The article doesn't begin on the front page, because they never put articles there. But there is a blurb. It says, 'You may have seen this face before, any number of times. It belonged to Penelope Noble, twenty-seven, one of the stars of the Park Avenue social whirl, and a rising young executive with the world's biggest soap company. Penelope was a debutante, a graduate of a prestigious women's college, and a tireless crusader with the Junior League. We say was, because Penelope was savagely murdered last night along with Harris Cohn, a two-bit pusher and pornographer, in Cohn's tawdry townhouse apartment. What was this noble woman doing with a low-life like Cohn? That mystery is currently under investigation. Story and pictures inside.' "

Melanie began to cry, her sobs resembling her laughter. Both were little waves of chirps that sounded almost like Melanie was hyperventilating. Lisa considered trying to comfort her, to tell her that everything would be all right, but instead said nothing; she decided that it was good for Melanie to cry, and almost wished that she would start to cry too.

"I'm sorry, Lisa," Melanie said haltingly, "Let me get a Kleenex." The phone was silent for a brief second. When Melanie returned, she continued, "I shouldn't have asked you to read any of it. I don't want to hear any more."

"That's okay, Mel. It's okay." She was relieved that she didn't have to read the rest of the story to Melanie, because it only got worse. There were four stories about the murder on pages 2 and 3. One dealt exclusively with the details of the double homicide, one was a brief biography of Harris Cohn, and two were about Penny Noble—one about her "society" wedding the previous fall, and one about her "fast-track" career with Dayton-Patterson. There were plenty of photographs as well. One of them, so grainy Lisa could barely make out the details, was of the "lovers' bodies" being carried from Cohn's apartment.

"I just hate newspapers," Melanie said. "They can be so mean and unfair."

"They can also be wrong. At least in this case. For instance, the *Post* says she was married in September instead of November, and that she was head of some

Junior League anticrack committee, when I think she quit the whole organization a year and a half ago. They also say she's been working at Dayton-Patterson one year, and I know that's not true. She's been there since she finished business school—and that was almost three years ago."

"Lisa, who cares about things like the date of her wedding? What was she doing with a pornographer? What was he to her?"

"Things like whether she was married in September or November are trivial points," Lisa went on, "but to screw it up shows a certain sloppiness. I'll bet they weren't really concerned about the facts. Which is why I'm not sure about how much of all this to believe."

"But she was with a pornographer."

"And a pimp and a drug dealer. But at least they're all the same guy. And if you read the *Times*, you also see he's only an alleged pimp and drug dealer."

"Read me the *Times* then," Melanie said, blowing her nose.

"You're sure you want me to?"

"I can't stand that other garbage. I can't. But I have to know what happened."

Lisa neatly folded the *New York Post* and pushed it to a far corner of her desk. She quickly scanned the *Times* until she found the Lord & Taylor maillot advertisement. Next to the ad was a long column of news blurbs.

"It's a short article on page 11, 'Two Dead in Village Apartment.' It's only three paragraphs.

"'Two adults, a man and a woman, were murdered early Wednesday night in an apartment in a Greenwich Village townhouse. The man, thirty-five-year-old Harris Cohn, died of multiple bullet wounds. The woman, twenty-seven-year-old Penelope Noble, was shot repeatedly in the body, but appears to have died as the result of head injuries sustained in a beating.

"'According to Manhattan Detective Richard Heckler, the murders may have been drug-related since Mr. Cohn, a

photographer, had been under investigation for drug traf-
ficking. The victims were found at 10:30 P.M. last night in
Mr. Cohn's apartment on 319 Garrett Street.

" 'Mrs. Noble, of 945 Park Avenue in Manhattan, had
no apparent connection to Mr. Cohn. She was an executive with the Dayton-Patterson Company in New
York City, in charge of its Whisper Soap business. Police
are now trying to determine why she was at his apartment Wednesday night.'

"That's the *Times* account," Lisa concluded glumly,
tossing the newspaper on to the metal credenza behind
her.

"In some ways," Melanie said, "it's worse than the
New York Post. The *Times* managed to reduce the whole
thing to three paragraphs. A woman is murdered, and
her death is condensed to one hundred words."

"A man and a woman were murdered," Lisa said,
correcting her.

"I don't care about the man."

Lisa smiled faintly and looked down at her desk calendar, hoping to find on it an excuse to get off the
phone. Sometimes Melanie was best in small doses. She
saw, however, a blank day, and unwilling to lie to
Melanie, asked simply, "What time will you be here
tonight?"

"I'm going to try for the six P.M. shuttle, but a lot
will depend on traffic. So I may be on the one at seven.
Are you going to call Christine?"

"I don't have to. She already knows."

"She already knows? How come?"

"She's in New York right now," Lisa answered,
pressing her thumb and forefinger down haphazardly on
her desk blotter, studying the black fingerprints. "At
Penny and Gordon's apartment, as a matter of fact. We
were all going to have dinner tonight. She's been visiting
them—was visiting them—since Monday."

"Oh God, how awful for her!"

"She's sounded better, that's for sure. I talked to her

about an hour ago, when I called to ask Gordon about the funeral arrangements. She was on phone duty for him. And Penny's family.''

"Those poor people, reporters must be driving them crazy. Just hounding them. People who don't care about Gordon's feelings, or Penny's parents' feelings. People who want to make this out to be as dirty as possible.''

"You're probably right, Mel,'' Lisa said thoughtfully, looking in her top desk drawer for a copy of *New York* magazine. "Penny's family is being hounded, and the stuff being written about Penny is terrible.''

"And the thing that's so frustrating is that we can't do anything about it.''

Lisa flipped through the front pages of the magazine until she found the masthead. "Well, that's not altogether true,'' she said, writing down the publication's telephone number. "Maybe I'm no better than a *Post* reporter for even suggesting this, but what would you think if I wrote an article about Penny? Sort of a 'this was the real Penny Noble' kind of thing. You know, you've read them—an anatomy of how Penny wound up in this Cohn guy's apartment. What led up to it. *New York* magazine always has pieces like that.''

"Lisa, how could you?'' Melanie asked softly, again close to tears. "How can you even consider writing a story about one of your oldest friends?''

"That's the main reason I want to, Mel. Because we were such good friends. I would love to be able to write something to shut up the tabloids. Write about the Penny we knew, make it clear that she wasn't some drug addict or prostitute. I would interview you, I would interview Christine, I would talk to her Junior League buddies. I could even talk to her business friends at Dayton-Patterson. They're a client, you know.''

"You and Penny worked together? You never told me!''

"No, Melanie, we never worked together. Dayton-Patterson is only one of about fifteen or twenty accounts in this agency, and I've never worked on it. But I do know the D-P account executives pretty well, including the guy who worked with Penny. So I'm in as good a position as anyone to write about Penny. To save her reputation. Her memory.''

"I just don't think it's a good idea," Melanie said. "I think Gordon and Penny's parents would rather see the whole thing just fade away.''

"Fine," Lisa said, not wanting to fight with Melanie. "Do you have a place to stay in New York?"

"I'll be okay. I think I'll call a guy I know in Hoboken. A musician who plays Boston clubs a lot. Marty Misery.''

"Marty Misery? What kind of name is that?"

"It's his stage name, I guess.''

"Melanie, you guess?"

"Well, I'm ninety-nine percent sure. He's the lead singer of Marty Misery and the Earwigs. I've always called him Marty, so his real name has never come up.''

"So you two just met at some club?"

"No, of course not. I'm designing some publicity posters for his band, and a cover for their first album. Honest, Marty's for real.''

"Why don't you stay at my place, Melanie? We'll both be happier.''

"But where would you stay? Your studio is tiny.''

"I spend almost every weekend at Mark's anyway. He has a nice, big, roomy apartment. It's a one-bedroom, but palatial next to my place.''

"Well, if you're sure you don't mind . . .''

"Not a bit," Lisa said, "I don't mind at all. Why don't you come straight to my apartment as soon as your plane lands, and then we'll go out to dinner. Or better yet, can we pick a place for dinner now and just meet there? Save a step?''

"Sure, that's okay. I'll only have an overnight bag.''

"Good. How does McSweet's sound?"

"I've never been there.''

"I think you'll like it. Mark will probably join us, but I wouldn't count on Christine. I think she'll probably be with Gordon or Penny's parents."

"You know, Lisa," Melanie sighed, "the one good thing to come out of all this is that you and me and Christine will all be together again. I'm really looking forward to that."

"I am too," Lisa said. "I really am."

3

Why Richard Heckler Couldn't Finish His Egg McMuffin

Detective Richard Heckler could not finish his Egg McMuffin. The photographs of Penelope Noble and Harris Cohn were that bloody. He had a dozen of them on his desk, the black-and-white glossies the police had taken the night before in Cohn's living room. And bedroom. And front hall. Those two had been fighters, Heckler thought to himself, no doubt about it. Especially the woman. Cohn had been killed first, it appeared, in the bedroom, but the woman had managed to fight her way into the front hall, dying finally within inches of the front door. Some rookie cop had actually begun examining the trajectory of the bullets, before realizing that it was not only hopeless, it was meaningless. It was clear from the blood—and the actual trails of blood—that Cohn and Noble had been shot first in the living room, but not fatally. Cohn had broken for the bedroom, and Noble for the front door. A Saturday night special had been emptied into them, and all six bullets accounted for: two in Cohn, four in Noble. Amazingly, it wasn't the bullet wounds that had killed Noble. Evidently out of bullets, the killer had had to smash in her skull with a steel espresso maker as she crawled to the door. It astounded Heckler that no one in the building heard anything, but then, no one in New York ever seemed to hear anything. Especially when there was a murder.

If anything about the case surprised Heckler, it was the fact that whoever had killed Noble and Cohn was a rank amateur. He had to admit it, when he had arrived at Cohn's townhouse the night before, he had expected to find the work of professionals. Organized crime rubbing out a small-time coke dealer and pornographer who was behind in his payments. A not uncommon scenario. But these murders were as unprofessional as they came, violent, unplanned, and sloppy. It was clear that whoever had killed Noble and Cohn had had no idea what he was doing.

It was also clear that Noble or Cohn had known the man who would kill them. There was no sign of forced entry, they had let him in the door themselves.

Heckler ran his hand across his hair, a razor cut of black bristles. The mark of the Astor Place barbershop. It was obvious to him that a key part of his investigation would be figuring out what the hell a Park Avenue socialite was doing with a low-life like Harris Cohn. Which would mean interviewing half of *Avenue* magazine and the Junior League. So in the interest of furthering the investigation, he pulled off his red leather string tie and reached into his desk for his navy blue rep. If he was going to interview the Social Register, he better not look like a bouncer at the Palladium.

4

A Barren Hermaphrodite

By the time Lisa hung up the phone with Melanie, it was almost noon. Her office, with its four beige metal walls and two gray metal filing cabinets, seemed unusually gloomy and claustrophobic. Especially after her dream the night before. Her nightmare. Certainly it was just a coincidence, but good God, she thought, what a macabre one. To dream of Penny the night Penny was murdered, after having not really thought about the woman in months. To dream of Penny's death. She found herself taking some comfort in the fact that the dream and the murder occurred hours apart, but it was still quite creepy.

She decided she had to leave the agency for the day, get out, go home. Clearly she wasn't going to get a whole lot done. At least not a whole lot that was particularly productive.

Only as a concession to the company, therefore, a sop to her own inordinate work ethic, she told herself she would devote fifteen minutes before leaving to making piles: she would clear out her in box. Reduce that one big pile into a series of little ones. One pile would be for legal correspondence: her agency's new toilet paper commercial had been approved by ABC and NBC, but CBS wanted further substantiation for their claim that the brand was the most absorbent tissue available ("the bathroom sponge"). Another pile was soon built out of conference reports with her client, recapitulations of what they talked about on the phone yesterday and when they had met the week before in Cincinnati (discussing the market research study that proved conclusively, via in-home testing, that their toilet paper really was the most absorbent).

When she was through, she had reduced the one big pile into a series of little ones, each ready to be dropped neatly into the color-coated hanging Pendaflex files in her two gray filing cabinets. Soon the top of her desk was bare, a wood-finish metal wasteland broken only by a mushroom desk lamp at one end and a mushroom paperweight at the other. The lamp looked to most people like a breast, while the paperweight reminded others of testicles. The desk was a hermaphrodite. When Lisa was finished, it was a barren hermaphrodite.

She looked at her desk, sad and unsatisfied. It was clean, she had a clean desk. As always, she had completed her job with the thoroughness of a demolitions expert, collapsing the one big pile her secretary dumped in her in-box into a series of manageable little stacks. Some had her harried scribbling on them. Others had little yellow stickies with route lists, so other people could scribble on them. That, essentially, was her job. Making little piles.

And when she was through, Penny Noble was still dead.

She slipped her three city newspapers into her attaché case and wiped the ink off her finger tips with her handkerchief. She dropped a note on her secretary's desk saying she was catching some sort of flu, and started home.

Halfway to the elevator, however, she stopped and turned toward Warren Racine's office. Warren was the account executive on Whisper, the Dayton-Patterson beauty soap, meaning he had been Penny Noble's contact at the agency.

Warren was leaning against his desk, laughing with someone on the phone. Warren was a tall, thin fellow who always wore suspenders and bow ties; he believed—by his own admission—that he really deserved the life promised in premium beer commercials. When he saw Lisa, he stoped giggling and hung up quickly. Lisa noticed that the *New York Post* and *Daily News* on his blotter were both opened to stories about Penny Noble.

"Lisa," he began immediately, "I am so sorry about your friend. All of us in the account group are."

"All right, Warren, fess up," Lisa said, more irritated by his ridiculous condolences than by the fact that he had been joking about Penny's death. "What was so funny?"

"When? Just now?"

"Yes, just now. I know you were laughing about Penny's murder. You were making some sick joke."

He put his hands in his pants pockets and looked down at his feet. "Look, I know there's nothing funny about Penny Noble being dead. I am as sorry as anyone about that. And just as sad. But good God, who in the world would have picked Penny to be involved in this sort of thing?"

"What 'sort' of thing?"

"Jeez, Lisa, I don't know exactly. But you know what I mean. All this innuendo about drugs and pornography. It just doesn't sound like the Penny Noble I knew. I mean, the woman was a walking commercial for Brooks Brothers, and Talbot's, and L. L. Bean. She was an MBA from Columbia, for crying out loud, not a crack addict!"

"Is that what people are saying?"

"That Penny Noble was a crack addict? No, no, no, of course not. But no one knows what to say. People are just—well, let's be kind—a tad perplexed."

"They're making jokes."

"No. I'm making jokes. Just me. The kind of guy who eulogizes Christa McAuliffe and Liberace with limericks. So if you want to get mad, just get mad at me."

"I'm not mad at you, Warren," Lisa said, her voice suddenly cracking. "I'm just . . . I'm in shock too. And now everyone is saying all these terrible things about her that just aren't true." She stumbled into his office, identical to hers except for the desk lamp, and collapsed in the chair before him. "Maybe I am mad, Warren," she went on, trying to prevent herself from breaking down in front of him, "but not at you. At everyone. Right now I'm mad at everyone."

Warren nodded. "Can I get you a glass of water?"

"No."

"A cup of tea? I could run down to the cafeteria."

"No, but that's sweet of you."

"What then? What can I do for you? You must have come by here for a reason."

"Yeah, I did," she said, taking a deep breath. "I want the names of the people Penny worked with at D-P."

"What are you doing, putting together a memorial service?"

"No, I hadn't thought of that. But that would be a nice thing to do."

"Then what?"

"This will probably sound moronic right now, because I haven't thought it all the way through yet. But I want to write an article about Penny. I want to find out what she was really doing with Harris Cohn last night, and salvage her reputation. Does that sound stupid?"

Warren folded his arms across his chest. "Yes, Lisa, it does. I'm sorry, but that just doesn't sound real smart."

"Why?"

"Because that's why we have police. To find out what Penny Noble was doing with Harris Cohn. And if it was innocent, people will be told."

"By whom? The tabloids? No way, Warren. They'll only have follow-ups on this story if she really does turn out to be a moonlighting porno queen!"

"The *Times* then. Or television. But I promise, if Penny had a valid reason for being at this Harris Cohn guy's place Wednesday night, people will hear about it."

"That's bullshit, Warren, it's just not true!" Lisa said. "This is only news if my friend is a tramp! Or a drug addict! And she wasn't either. I really knew her. No reporter can say that. I lived with her for four years. I had been her friend for ten. That's why I want to write this article."

"And you want to interview people at D-P?"

"That's right."

"I think that's a bad idea."

"Why?"

"Are you serious?" Warren asked, almost laughing. "You know D-P. We're talking about a very uptight company, Lisa, very straitlaced. These are the kind of people who shit in rows."

"So?"

"Get a clue, Lisa. D-P does not want any more publicity out of this than they've already gotten. It's happened, and they're sad, but now it's over. Now they just want the whole story to fade away. Just disappear."

"All I want to do is ask some of her associates some innocuous questions."

"There is nothing innocuous about a murdered D-P brand manager."

"So you're saying no one there will talk to me?"

"Right."

"Well, why don't you give me some names so I can find that out for myself?"

"I'm sorry, I can't do that. I don't want to piss anyone off."

"Are *you* serious?"

"Uh-huh."

"Where's your spine?"

Warren tried to meet Lisa's eyes and smile, but failed. "No need to get nasty," he said, looking over at a filing cabinet.

"I could get some names by just calling the D-P switchboard," Lisa told him. "But I was hoping you could save me some trouble."

"I'm trying to save you trouble, Lisa. I really am. You don't want to interview D-P personnel. All that will happen is they'll get mad at you, and then they'll get mad at the agency, and then the agency will get mad at you. And they won't tell you squat. I promise you that. They won't tell you squat."

Lisa stared at the front of his desk for a long, quiet moment, fuming. Finally she got up to leave, and said to him, "You've been a very big help. Thank you. You're just a prince."

Warren shrugged, looking down at his wingtips. "I'm sorry," he mumbled, "but trust me: you don't want to talk to D-P. You just don't."

5

Teddies and Tap Pants

Heckler had no rational reason for interviewing Penny Noble's friends before Harris Cohn's. He told himself it was because he had to find out what Noble was doing with Cohn, but he didn't really believe that this was the quickest route to the killer. After all, whoever had killed them had come for Cohn, and Penny Noble had just happened to be in the wrong place at the wrong time. Had to be. Still, Noble's friends were probably more interesting than Cohn's associates (and they would certainly be more talkative), so he decided to begin his investigation uptown. He began with Christine Yarbrough, since she appeared to be the last person to have seen Penny Noble alive, other than the murderer himself.

The woman who greeted Heckler at the door to the Nobles' apartment Thursday afternoon caught him off guard. She was larger than he was, no small feat given Heckler's own bulk. Instead of the trim, classically tailored female executive he had expected, he was met by a hulking, overweight woman in a tattered blue sweatshirt.

A woman so fat that in spite of her sweatshirt, he could tell that her elbows were covered with the same bouncy sponge cakes of cellulite that puffed out her blue jeans like jodhpurs.

"I'm Richard Heckler," he told the woman casually. "And you're Christine Yarbrough?"

"That's right. Please come in."

"I'm very sorry about your friend, Ms. Yarbrough, and I understand this is a very difficult time for you," Heckler said, the speech second nature to him. He knew it as well as the Miranda rights. "But the time we spend together now could be very helpful."

"You don't have to apologize to me," Christine said, her voice betraying a southern accent with a surprisingly hard edge. "I understand. The ones who need your 'I'm so sorries' are Gordon and Penny's parents."

Heckler quickly scanned the Nobles' apartment, wondering if the small painting above the fireplace was a real Renoir. "You did tell me Mr. Noble wouldn't be home, didn't you?"

"Sure did. He's with Penny's family, over on Fifth. Want some coffee?"

Heckler nodded, and Christine wandered into the kitchen. "It'll be instant," she hollered out to him. "Make yourself at home. I have."

Heckler sat down in the living room, noting that at some point Christine had taken the Nobles' telephone off the hook.

When Christine returned, she sat across from him on the couch and said, "I'll bet you see a lot of this."

"Murder?"

She frowned. "No, instant coffee. 'Course I mean murder. This all must be pretty run of the mill to you."

"No way. Especially not this one." Heckler sipped his coffee, wondering briefly if he should begin with very specific questions about Penny Noble's last hours or more general ones about the woman herself. He usually liked to begin with generalities, but Christine Yarbrough seemed very tough and straightforward. On the other hand, the two women had been good friends—college roommates, in fact—so Heckler opted to start with some broad-stroke inquiries. "Were you and Ms. Noble close?" he asked, staring down at the coffee table.

"Call her Penny," Christine said. "Yeah, I guess we were close. We hadn't seen each other much since college, but I guess we were still sorta close. Some things don't change."

"Any special reason you hadn't seen each other much lately?"

"Nope. I just moved back to Atlanta, and Penny lived here. That's all."

"What do you do in Atlanta?" Heckler asked, not particularly interested, but hoping to relax Christine by getting the woman to talk about herself for a moment. But the ploy backfired.

"What's that got to do with my friend's murder?" Christine asked tensely.

"Nothing. I'm just curious."

Christine shook her head irritably, and Heckler noticed for the first time the gray in her dark hair. "If you must know—and I don't know why you must—I manage a Hallmark card store. One near Peachtree. Don't ask me what I'm doing running it, 'cause I'm not altogether sure I know myself. I just fell into it when I decided I didn't want to be a lawyer, and dropped outta Emory."

"Don't apologize."

"Don't think I did."

Heckler grinned and reached into his blazer pocket for a toothpick. He knew it was a disgusting habit, but it was better than smoking. "When did you arrive in New York?"

"Monday."

"And you've been staying here ever since?"

"All three days, yup."

"Did Ms. Noble—Penny—ever mention Harris Cohn in that time?"

"Nope, not once."

"Had she ever mentioned him? Had you ever heard of him?"

"Nope, and nope again. First I heard his name was about eleven o'clock last night, when Gordon mumbled it. He had just heard from your buddies downtown that they'd found Penny."

"Do you have any idea why she might have been with Harris Cohn?"

Christine snorted. "I don't have a clue. Not the foggiest notion at all."

"Do you know if Penny was involved with drugs? Cocaine, maybe?"

"Yeah, I guess it's possible. It ain't likely, but it's possible."

"Did you two do any stuff this week?"

"Oh, ain't we abrupt," Christine said, arching her eyebrows. "No, Detective Heckler, we didn't."

"Could she have been scoring something from Cohn? For a friend, perhaps?"

"Sure, that's possible too, but I don't imagine it's the case."

"Want to tell me about your last hours together? Wednesday afternoon?"

"Do I have a choice?"

Heckler sat back on the couch, smiling. "Of course you have a choice. But I don't see why you wouldn't want to help us catch your friend's killer."

"I'm just not wild about your attitude," Christine said slowly, thoughtfully. "You make it sound like Penny was up to no good. Did she do 'stuff'? Was she 'scoring' something? Jesus H. Christ, Penny wasn't into that kinda thing."

"I'm sorry. But I need to learn about your friend."

"She wasn't a cokehead, that's for sure."

"Okay, fine. Point noted. What happened yesterday afternoon?"

Christine reached into the pocket across the front of

her sweatshirt and pulled out a pack of Parliaments. She offered one to Heckler, but he shook his head no and tapped his finger against his toothpick to explain why.

"Well, Gordon was working late last night," Christine began after she had lit her cigarette, "so Penny and I figured on doing some shopping, since most stores up here seem to be open a little late too. We started out at Altman's and were going to work our way uptown. At least that was our plan. But instead of going north, we went west. We went to Macy's after Altman's, and then to that mall. Herald Square, I think it's called."

"What time was all this?"

"I guess we left Altman's about five-thirty, maybe quarter to six. We hung out in Macy's for a long time, a good hour I'd bet. Which would have made it about seven when we left. And we only spent a little while together in the mall."

"And then what?"

"We split up. I came back here."

"How come?"

"If you must know, because I got rotten feet. They hurt like a bitch if I'm on 'em too long, and they were hurtin' something fierce last night. So I just apologized to Penny and came home."

Heckler glimpsed quickly down at Christine's feet, amazed at how small they were. No wonder they hurt: carting around Christine's body on those size fives must have been like moving a mobile home with a wheelbarrow. "How come she didn't go with you?"

"She wasn't done shopping. We were looking for a present for Gordon, and she hadn't found it yet. His birthday is next week, you see."

"What was she looking for?"

"I knew you'd get around to that," Christine said, almost lightly. "To be perfectly straight with you, I was glad my feet hurt. I mean, they really did, but I was looking for an excuse to split. Penny was buying herself a whole new lingerie wardrobe, you see, real sexy stuff.

That was going to be her present to Gordon. Herself in all this sexy teddy stuff. Gordon is a little uptight, understand, and she thought this might loosen him up. Don't get me wrong, their marriage was terrific and all. Penny just wanted to get a little, you know, randy.

"So we went to Altman's, expecting to begin there, but they didn't have much we liked. So Penny suggested we hit Macy's, since they have a real big lingerie department. At least that's what she said. So we went west instead of north. 'Cause of Macy's. Anyway, I was getting pretty darn sick of hanging out in underwear departments while Penny disappeared into dressing rooms with teddies, and tap pants, and ten million bras at a time. I was getting a little depressed just standing there, watching Penny pull all that stuff off the rack. She's always been in real good shape, and had a real cute figure, and I'm—well, you can see what I am. I've always felt like a bit of a pig around Penny.

"So when my feet hurt, I left," Christine continued, her speech slowing. "I just left. I said I'd meet her back here, and that . . . that was the last time I saw her."

"That was in Herald Square?"

"Yup. In a lingerie store on one of the upper levels," Christine said softly. "I don't remember the name."

"Did she say what time she would be home?"

"No, but I figured soon enough. I sure didn't figure she'd never come home." To Heckler she looked as if she might be close to tears.

"Do you know about what time you left her?" he asked gently.

"Seven-thirty. Maybe twenty to eight. Can I ask you a question for a change?"

"Sure you can," Heckler said, spreading his arms expansively.

"If I hadn't left Penny, what do you think would have happened?"

Heckler knew it was a rhetorical question. Christine was trying to convince herself that she was responsible for Penny's death. "Don't punish yourself," he told her. "You didn't kill Penny Noble."

"If I hadn't left her alone, she might still be alive."

"Or you might be dead too."

Christine shrugged, unwilling, it seemed to Heckler, to let herself off the hook.

As soon as Heckler left the Nobles' Park Avenue apartment, he went to Lexington to find a pay phone. He had considered calling the station from the Nobles', but he didn't want to upset Christine any more than he already had.

When he found a phone kiosk, on Lexington and Eighty-second Street, he called Edgar Burton, the crime scene investigator. Burton had joined him the night before at Cohn's townhouse and had spent much of the morning going over his findings with the medical examiner. While the dispatcher rang Burton, Heckler snuggled deeper into the kiosk, hoping to avoid as much of the cold April rain as he could.

"How do, Mr. Burton, what's the good word?" Heckler asked the ID man when he came on the line. "Been slam-dancing through lunch?" Heckler liked Burton, but he also liked tormenting him: Burton had to be one of the least interesting, most suburban guys he had ever met. Two kids, a house on the Island, an above-ground pool from Sears.

"No, Richard, I haven't been slab-dancing. I don't even know what slab-dancing is."

"So tell me," Heckler said, pulling up the collar of his raincoat, "any news?"

"Uh-huh. There were three sets of fresh prints at Cohn's, two of which have been positively identified as those of the victims. The third is no one we know, but we did find his prints on the espresso pot, one of the wine glasses, and the front door."

"What about the hair we found?"

"Five strands, definitely not Harris Cohn's or Penelope Noble's. Type A blood, matches one of the stains found on the living-room floor."

"So our killer is wounded."

"Not likely. Cut, scraped maybe. But nothing serious."

"Still, it helps. What about the victims' blood? Any signs of drugs or alcohol?"

"Cohn was completely clean. There was a very small trace of alcohol in the woman's system. Point-oh-five percent."

"But no drugs."

"No drugs. We did find powder traces in a closet, however, which we think is coke. It's being analyzed right now."

"Enough to suggest he was dealing?"

"Not really. But whoever killed Cohn may have taken the bulk of his junk with him."

"So is that the scoop?"

"Nope. I haven't told you my big news."

"Really big, Edgar?"

"Really big."

"Mondo big?"

"Look, you want me to tell you?" Burton asked, exasperated. "Then just listen: there was a roll of film in Cohn's camera, in his studio. Thirty-six exposures, black and white. You'll never guess who was on it."

"I probably won't, Edgar, so tell me."

"Penelope Noble."

Heckler nodded reflexively in the kiosk, as if Burton were telling him in person. "Is that a fact?"

"That's a fact. And do you know what she was wearing?"

It was clear from the lecherous excitement in Burton's voice that it wasn't a down parka. "A cheerleader's skirt," Heckler said, teasing him.

"Is that your guess?"

"That's my guess."

"Wrong. Guess again."

"Okay. Let's see, I bet she was wearing a black garter belt."

"That's close, Richard. But it was white. And she was wearing a teddy in some. And just—just heels in some others. How did you know?"

"I just talked to Christine Yarbrough. The college roommate. Or a college roommate, I should say. And she said that the last place she went to with Penny was a lingerie store."

"What else did she tell you?"

"Mostly just other names to talk to. Some other college friends coming to New York tonight, some who already live here. Want to get me the address of a woman named Lisa Stone? And her phone number?"

"That's not my job."

"Could you ask someone to, Edgar? Please?"

"Yes, Richard. That I can do."

"Thank you, Edgar," Heckler said. "I'll never, ever forget you for this."

6

The Shirt with Pink Palm Trees

It was drizzling outside when Lisa left the agency for the day, half-frozen April raindrops falling like gravel. She knew she wouldn't find a cab, not at the tail end of lunch hour, not in the rain. So she opened her briefcase, hoping to discover an umbrella hidden beneath her newspapers, but all she found were two pens and a solar-powered calculator: she had organized her briefcase the night before, and no piles had survived. Angry with herself, she began the six-block walk to the subway.

To some extent, the storm struck her as a kind of justifiable punishment. It had been occurring to Lisa with increasing frequency that she was too damn compulsive. Her mother was a math teacher and her father an architect, and from them she had inherited a desire for organization that was almost unnatural. Or at least excessive.

Mark, after all, seemed perfectly content amidst his disarray. So had all her other lovers since college. They had all been slobs. As she crossed Lexington Avenue, avoiding a puddle in the crosswalk, she realized that not once had she slept with a man who put down the toilet seat after peeing. It was almost as if she unconsciously sought out partners who were her opposite: men as spontaneous as she was systematic, as undisciplined as she was directed, as unconcerned as she was compulsive. Mark Scher was a perfect example. And yet they had been dating for six months now, and Lisa was wonderfully happy with him.

They had met at Penny's wedding to Gordon Noble the previous Thanksgiving, because he had been the one person in the Colony Club ballroom who looked rumpled. He was more sloppy than slobby: the top button of his blue Oxford shirt was undone, and the tail of his necktie dangled as prominently as the front; although the same rain was falling equally on all guests, only Mark's shoes were stained by street ash, rock salt, soot, and mud; and while many people there wore glasses, only Mark kept his perched on his nose with a piece of folded Scotch Tape. Mark, a dark-haired thirty-one-year-old attorney, had never been married, but nevertheless radiated the sort of calm assurance and tranquility usually associated only with happily married men. Lisa spent almost the entire reception with him, comparing notes about the bride and groom: Mark knew Gordon from the University Club, but had spent very little time with Penny; Lisa, on the other hand, had known Penny very well at Crosby (although they had seen less and less of each other since graduating), but had met Gordon only twice. They both agreed that neither would have had a good time at the reception without the other.

It was almost two o'clock by the time she reached the subway entrance at Fifty-first Street. She paused at the corner, wondering whether she should cross the street as she planned and take the downtown train home. Downtown was Greenwich Village. Although the Village was fifteen wide blocks south of her home, it was a presence to her that crept up to the front door of her building. It was a grainy presence born of dead lovers' bodies, shadowy faces with translucent, sparkling eyes, and stoned specters making love for Harris Cohn, filmmaker. She couldn't go downtown.

The idea of going uptown to Mark's apartment instead, and waiting for him, was much more appealing. Mark at that moment was returning from a conference in Houston, with his plane due to land at La Guardia at four-thirty. Which meant he would not in all likelihood go to his office. Not on a rainy Thursday. He would go straight home. And he would find her in his bed in his apartment, a pleasant surprise until she told him she was there because she was afraid to go home, that she was sad and scared and angry all at once.

She descended the uptown entrance, trying to remember what clothing she had at Mark's, and then not caring. She knew there was a lot of it, and all she was interested in at that moment anyway was his flannel bathrobe.

While sitting in her corner seat on the subway she tried to find Harris Cohn. Yes, he was dead, but what did he look like? Was he a white version of the middle-aged black man whose paunch flopped over his genitals toward the plastic seat before him? Or was he more like the young man in the red plaid suit and gold bracelet, in all likelihood an insurance salesman for New York or Prudential or Metropolitan? Or was he most like the tall, thin college student in a Hawaiian shirt, painter's pants, and Ray-Bans? Yes, that was Harris Cohn, older, heavier, but the type who wore Ray-Bans on subways. She was not sure if Mr. Ray-Ban was staring at her or at the Woolite bathing beauty above her, but the steady gaze of his sunglasses began to frighten her. She wasn't just self-conscious: she was intimidated. It was unreasonable, she knew it, but when the train reached Seventy-seventh Street, she bolted up the steps.

When she entered Mark's building on Eightieth Street she nodded at the doorman and was struck by her reflection in the mirrors behind him. She was surprised at how pale she had become. Her skin, normally a healthy khaki, was white. Even her eyes seemed to be a paler blue than they usually were. She saw also that her hair looked comical, a thin sandy mat that stuck to her head like a bathing cap. She wished she had not had so much chopped off the other day.

Mark lived on the fifteenth floor of a dreary apartment built in the early 1960s. It was designed as middle-income housing, but as the result of the escalation in rents and real-estate values in Manhattan, the building had evolved into a luxury co-op. Mark's one-bedroom was much larger than Lisa's Gramercy Park studio, but Lisa thought it lacked the studio's eclectic charm. His walls were sensibly flat, while hers were crisscrossed with protruding deco beams and circuitous snakes of plaster masonry. All charm in Mark's home depended upon the amount and the quality of the visible clutter: open broken-spined books, empty coffee mugs, and piles of dry-cleaned clothes.

His apartment that afternoon was in typical condition. A four-day-old Sunday *Times* rested by the television. The sweater he had worn the previous weekend was in a crumpled ball by the drop-leaf table. Five or six Hertz bills were stacked on the glass coffee table, as was a Bloomingdale's catalogue and an invitation to join the Smithsonian. Two piles of clothing sat beside the couch, one clean, one dirty. After briefly surveying the apartment, Lisa hung up her clothing in the bathroom, discovering that even her lingerie was saturated. Reflexively, she reached over and put down the cover on the toilet. When she had hung everything neatly on the bar over the bathtub, she folded herself into the flannel robe hanging behind the bathroom door and collapsed atop his unmade bed. Suddenly, all she wanted to do was sleep.

Lisa was awakened from a dream later that afternoon, when she felt a hand on her shoulder. In her dream it was Harris Cohn's hand, because it was attached to a shirt packed with pink palm trees and parakeets. She jumped in her sleep, opened her eyes, and was relieved to discover that it was Mark's hand. And then she began to cry. All at once her eyes were tearing and her nose was running, and although she wasn't sobbing out loud, her body shook like it was. Everything that had been welling up inside her all day began to come out, and it came out all over Mark's suit.

"Shhh," Mark whispered, rocking her gently. "Shhh."

"Penny's dead," Lisa managed to tell him through her sniffles.

"I know. I know all about it. I saw the newspapers at the airport."

Lisa tried to rationalize her outburst, attributing it first to premenstrual syndrome and then to exhaustion. Neither made a whole lot of sense, however; Lisa knew she was crying for Penny, and this made her angry. Because her tears were not merely tears of loss (although that was certainly a big part of it), they were tears of guilt, tears of frustration. It was not just the fact that Penny Noble was dead that was abruptly pushing her to the brink of hysteria, or the fact that there was a part of her friend that she knew nothing about, a side to her she had never seen; rather, it was the way her friend had died and the way the tabloids were sensationalizing her death that was so upsetting. How could Penny have let it all happen? What was she up to?

"You know who must not be taking this whole thing particularly well," Mark said later, as he watched Lisa get dressed again, "is ol' Gordo Noble."

She turned to him, holding in her hands a pair of wool pants she had worn New Year's Eve and a blouse from the previous weekend. "I think that's probably an understatement. Of course he's not taking it well, she was his wife."

"What I mean is, it would be one thing if she died in a car crash. It's another to be found dead with a pornographer. That one fact alone must be driving Gordon crazy. He has to be the straightest guy I've ever met. The type who can get pissed off just walking past X-rated movie marquees."

Lisa shrugged, wondering briefly what other clothing she had left at Mark's over the last half-year. "What do you think Penny was doing with that man? Was it drugs? Or was it an affair or something?"

"You knew her better than me. I don't have a clue."

"Did Gordon ever say anything about their marriage? Did they have a good marriage?"

"I couldn't tell you that either. Gordon never said anything to me that made me think they didn't. But then, I've only seen him twice since the wedding, and both times it was just to play squash."

Lisa nodded, disturbed by the idea that Gordon and Penny's marriage had been in trouble after only six months. She wished the thought hadn't even come to her. It wasn't right to think for even the slightest moment that Gordon could have had something to do with Penny's death, it just wasn't right. Unfortunately, Lisa couldn't get the idea out of her mind.

7

Gordon Noble's
Golden Girl

Lisa and Mark reached McSweet's a little after seven, well ahead of Melanie. Initially Lisa ordered a vodka tonic, but when Mark started using the crayons on the table to draw intravenous bags with tentacles, she decided she had better remain coherent and ordered a glass of wine instead. McSweet's, which once looked like a Victorian dance hall with warm, dark booths, had been redecorated. It now looked like an art deco cafeteria, lit dimly by life-size silhouettes of naked women holding planets, and all-black twin-engine propeller planes that hung from the ceiling. The tableclothes were white poster paper, and the menu flashed in orange and blue neon on opposite walls. The waiters and waitresses had identically cropped blond razor cuts and wore black eye shadow. Lisa decided she had been more comfortable with the red velour and tulip lamps of the old McSweet's.

By the time Melanie arrived, near eight o'clock, Lisa was on her second glass of wine and felt pleasantly dulled, despite her intentions. When Lisa saw her at the door, she panicked briefly, fearing that Melanie might have brought someone with her. Since Christmas, Melanie had been seeing a man who gave dogs cancer and put them to sleep. He was a scientist at M.I.T., but Lisa did not believe any number of credentials could have made him tolerable company that evening. By the time the idea had shot through Lisa, however, she saw that Melanie was alone.

Melanie's hair was black that day, instead of its natural dirty blond. Lisa recalled that the last time she had seen Melanie, it had been green. Melanie was wearing a short white dress, emboldened by long strips of graffiti: not actual words, but bold splashes of color. Her stockings were black, with white crosses and stars sewn up the seams. Her one earring was the swab from a vial of blue Liquid Paper.

Mark grabbed Lisa's wrist. Smirking, he whispered in an affected, nasal voice, "Cheeky, cheeky, cheeky. On the runway now is Melanie Braverman, a walking work of art. She is modeling the latest from Milan, titled Classical Subway." Mark had met Melanie twice before, and although he liked her, he had told Lisa that he thought she dressed like a music video.

Melanie glided across the bar to Lisa and Mark's table, kissing Lisa on the cheek, but sitting across from her beside Mark.

"You sounded so depressed on the phone this morning," she began, "that I was determined to be cheerful. So I stole this dress from a friend of mine, because it seemed perfect for New York. Demimonde, but tasteful."

Lisa did not remember sounding any more depressed than Melanie, and thought she may actually have sounded less so.

"A gallant gesture," Mark said.

"I think so," Melanie agreed.

After a waiter took her request for a spritzer, Melanie turned to Lisa and said, "I haven't eaten since lunch, so I'm famished."

"I haven't either. As the matter of fact, I haven't eaten since breakfast. A croissant. That's all I've had today. A croissant."

"You should eat something," Mark told her.

"You're right, I should. I just haven't been hungry." She turned to her friend, asking, "So, Melanie, how are you?"

"Until today, I was wonderful. I just don't understand what happened. What was she doing with that man?"

Lisa paused, surprised that Melanie had brought Penny up so quickly. She had known before she arrived at the restaurant that it would be Melanie who would first broach the subject of Penny's murder, but she had thought it would take Melanie at least one drink to get around to it.

"I don't know," she answered Melanie. "I don't know anything more this evening than I knew at eleven-thirty this morning." She liked the cold of the glass against her hand. It was hot in the restaurant, and the glass was soothing.

"Did you bring the newspapers with you?"

"No, I forgot them. They're at Mark's, so I can show them to you tomorrow."

"You don't really want to see them," Mark told her. "They're pretty graphic."

"I expect that. But I want to see them anyway. I loved Penny."

Lisa rolled her eyes at Melanie's liberal use of the word. The way Melanie defined love, it seemed sometimes that she was in love with half of New York and all of Boston. "Don't worry, you'll see them," she said. "Let's settle down for a moment."

When the waiter returned with Melanie's spritzer, she raised her glass, saying, "Well, cheers. What's the expression, Lisa, to absent friends?"

"Salud," Lisa said, nodding. She realized suddenly that tomorrow she and Christine and Melanie would all be together in one place without Penny. For one of the few times since college. She understood with an abrupt pang that Penny's death meant not only the end of her own individual friendship with that woman, it damaged irreparably the group friendship that had once existed among Lisa, Melanie, Christine, and Penny. Although the four women had grown apart since they had left Crosby, geographic differences exacerbating emotional ones, Lisa still felt that they were bound by certain shared memories. The Victorian house the four women had lived in on Nash Street in Winston their junior and senior years. Penny's three-year affair with Leslie Nichols, an overly sensitive, middle-aged male sociology professor. Christine's bulimia, which she finally beat, but which had left a once hauntingly beautiful young woman anywhere between seventy-five and one hundred pounds overweight. Lisa didn't believe that Penny was the only bond among the four women, but often she was the only personality among them kind enough to keep the warring factions at peace. And now that buffer zone was gone.

"I see you're not smoking," Lisa told Melanie at one point, after watching her crunch her ice cubes into clear little pebbles and then return them to her glass.

"Not this second. But I do have some in my purse. I must admit, I have been smoking a lot less since I started going out with William," Melanie said, referring to her boyfriend at M.I.T.

"It must be awfully tough to smoke around a cancer scientist," Mark said, nodding.

"It's impossible. Even if I had the desire, he wouldn't let me."

"You do seem to smoke less now than you did in college," Lisa said, simultaneously relieved and saddened for Melanie. Melanie had been such an attractive smoker. She would twirl a cigarette distractedly in her hand a long while before lighting it, and then, after exhaling the first time, hold her lips in a slight pucker. It always had struck Lisa as an extremely erotic gesture. Frivolous, perhaps affected, but sexy. "When you and Penny were together, you two could smoke out an auditorium in minutes."

"We were pretty heavy smokers. We used to smoke Marlboro 100s. Penny said we should have saved ourselves time and money and just machine-gunned our lungs."

"What was Penny like?" Mark asked Melanie. "I know Gordon, but I only met Penny a couple of times."

Melanie brought her glass to her lips, pausing. "Oh, I don't know. She always did things with more style than the rest of us. Like when she arrived at Crosby. While most eighteen-year-olds put up Bruce Springsteen posters or Hallmark puppies, she was putting up Edward Weston prints. Sexy peppers and toilets."

"Part of that is just that she always had better taste than most people, even as an eighteen-year-old," Lisa added.

"And more money, I'll bet," Mark suggested.

There was no malice in Mark's tone, but Lisa still thought that Penny should be defended. "That wasn't it, Mark. The only people at school who knew that Penny came from big bucks were those of us who knew her well. And the only one of us who even might have cared at all was Christine, and that's because she came from almost no money."

"I'm not saying she lorded anything over anyone. I know she wasn't like that," Mark said. "All I'm suggesting is that because she had more money, she may have had more style. It's the lawyer in me. I have to attribute everything to nurture."

"Ah, the rich are somehow different from you and me," Lisa said.

"Peter Gabriel," Melanie piped in, trying to source the reference.

"Close," she said, "Scott Fitzgerald." She then turned back to Mark, continuing, "Penny was also very sweet. That word isn't exactly right, because at least to me it always makes people sound like they're dim or boring. And Penny wasn't either."

"No, she was very smart," Melanie interjected. "And when we first met, for all of her sweetness and lace, she was also ambitious. A little aggressive, even."

"Like most Crosby freshmen, I suppose," Mark said.

"No, Penny was more than just a college go-getter,"

Lisa told him. "She just exuded this serene confidence. She always seemed to know exactly what she wanted, and you had this feeling she always got it."

"Sort of a golden girl, eh?" Mark wondered.

"Well, yes. Maybe. But then, she was a golden girl with a real knowing aura."

"Remember what Christine used to say about her?" Melanie asked, smiling.

"Not offhand."

"She used to say that Penny always had this 'freshly fucked' expression on her face!"

"That's funny," Mark said. "Was it true?"

"Was she always getting laid?" Melanie asked. "Remember, we are talking about a women's college. No freshman always got laid. But she probably had as much luck as anyone else who went through the place."

Lisa laughed, and put her hand on Mark's for a brief second. "I have to tell you, while Melanie was wasting her time getting groped at frat parties at other schools, and I was still trying to find my g-spot, our friend Penny was hanging out with assistant professors in their twenties and thirties."

"God, that wasn't my idea of Penny at all," Mark said, as the waiter returned to take their orders. "I had always assumed she was as uptight as Gordon."

When they had finished ordering, Lisa turned to Melanie and asked, "When did Penny start seeing Leslie? Was it sophomore fall or sophomore spring?"

"It had to be first semester, because the first time I saw them together was in the winter. Remember? Christine had just begun seeing the psychiatrist. I saw them twice. Once at a restaurant in North Adams and once in Boston, in a Newbury Street record store of all places."

"Leslie is the professor you've mentioned a couple of times, right?" Mark asked Lisa.

"Oh God, I hope I haven't," Lisa said, half-kidding. "And if I did, nothing I said can be held against me, because I must have been dead drunk."

Melanie smiled, her front teeth jutting forward like a beaver's. "You never told Mark about Professor Touchy-Feely?" she asked gleefully, seeming to revel in the memory.

"Not in detail, no."

"So tell me now," Mark said. "This sounds real juicy."

"There's nothing to tell," Lisa said, embarrassed. She was angry with herself for bringing Leslie up in the first place.

"I don't know, sounds awfully nasty to me," Mark said. "Why don't you tell me, Melanie?"

"Can I, Lisa?"

"Oh, for God's sake, it's just not that interesting," Lisa insisted. "Leslie's not that interesting. But if you must know, I'll tell you. First off, Professor Touchy-Feely was a nickname. Obviously. The guy's real name was Nichols. But we called him Professor Touchy-Feely because he was this very affected man who thought he had the world's most acute moral sensibility. He was a Crosby sociology professor who taught courses like 'The Urban Mystique' or the 'Uneasy Sexism of the Cree Indians.' I don't know when, but sometime he changed his name from Leonard to Leslie, because Leslie was androgynous."

"And he and Penny began this real steamy affair early in her sophomore fall," Melanie said.

"But we—at least Christine and me—didn't know about it until much later in the year. When she told us."

"Did they live together?" Mark asked.

"No," Melanie said. "Freshman and sophomore years she lived in Torrington House. With us. And then in our junior and senior years, the four of us lived together off campus, in that Victorian house on Nash Street."

"The red monster with the turrets," Lisa told him. "I think I've shown you pictures of it."

"You're right, you have," Mark said, sipping his drink. "How long were Penny and Leslie involved?"

"Until after we graduated. She stayed in Winston trying to keep it together for three or four months after we all left. But there was no way. No way at all. By then it was September, and already he was scouting his next lay."

"Sounds like a real charmer. What did Penny see in him?"

"The man was gorgeous," Melanie said. "He was one of the sexiest men I've ever met," she said in simple salute.

"Melanie is not exaggerating," Lisa said calmly. "He was—he is, I'm sure—one of the prettiest men around. He was in his mid to late thirties when we were at Crosby, and he had this dark blond hair that was just beginning to thin. And he had olive skin, but it wasn't greasy-looking olive. It was this perpetual tan kind of olive. He was also in great shape. He had played tennis at Berkeley—he was from San Francisco—and had never lost that tennis player's firmness."

"But it was his eyes that were the killers."

"Or how he used them," Lisa said, recalling them. "They were a very deep blue. Set back in that dark skin of his, they were eerie."

"He could really mesmerize a class with them," Melanie told Mark. "He could hypnotize ten of us in a seminar, or fifty of us in a lecture. It was a snap with those peepers."

"But let's face it," Lisa said, "the guy had every advantage possible. He was talking to eighteen-year-old women—no, girls, eighteen-year-old girls—who were vulnerable to that kind of sensitivity. Girls who picked a women's college specifically because they wanted to avoid the kind of male chauvinism found at most coed schools."

"Or because they didn't get into Yale," Melanie added.

"Besides," Lisa continued, ignoring Melanie, "his competition consisted almost exclusively of little boys from Williams College, and other women. We did see through him enough to call him Professor Touchy-Feely. But he was still very appealing to an eighteen-year-old."

There was a long pause while Mark waited for Lisa to continue. When she didn't, he spread out his arms and asked, "Is that it?"

"What did you expect?"

"By the way you and Melanie were talking, I expected something a lot juicier. A little intrigue. Some excitement, some competition. A threesome, maybe."

"Sorry," Lisa said. "No threesomes."

"She's not telling you the best part, Mark. Trust me."

"Melanie!"

"Oh, come on, Lisa, you should tell him. It was years ago!"

"Yes, Lisa, you should," Mark said. "I love the idea of finding a bit of tawdry dirt in your obsessively clean closet. Even if it is dirt that's a couple years old."

"Okay, fine," Lisa said, sitting back in her chair and folding her arms across her chest. "Once—one time— once, Leslie Nichols and I slept together."

"That's it?"

"That's it."

"Oh, you tramp, you," Mark teased.

"Satisfied?"

"No, not really. I was hoping for something worse. Sure it was only once?"

"Mark!"

"It really wasn't a big deal," Melanie added. "We all spent so much time in Leslie's house, hanging around with him, that it was bound to happen. I mean, I made love with Leslie once, too. So did Christine."

"What did Penny think about all this?" Mark asked.

"It just happened," Melanie said. "It didn't mean anything."

"Didn't it upset her? Wasn't she hurt?"

"Well, I guess she wasn't pleased," Melanie continued. "But everybody took it in stride. Either they weren't seeing each other for a while, or they had just had a fight, or we were all real stoned. But there was always an excuse."

"And I almost think Penny wanted Leslie to seduce us," Lisa explained. "Toward the end, she was willing to do anything to keep Leslie. I imagine in her eyes we were just an occasional extracurricular to keep him more or less monogamous."

"Sounds like a pretty high price," Mark said.

"Perhaps. But it didn't seem so then. It's like Melanie said. It just wasn't that big a deal at the time. It just happened. Okay?"

"Okay," Mark said. "Okay. But I have to tell you, I can't imagine the woman you've described marrying Gordon Noble."

"Why not?"

"Gordon is a funny guy, Lisa. He's real old-fashioned. Traditional. Especially when it comes to women. He struck me as the kind of guy who would want to marry some sexless, classy little Junior Leaguer. And I must admit, until tonight that was the impression I had of Penny Graves."

"What did Gordon say about her?"

"Not much, because we didn't really know each other all that well. But whenever he talked about her, I always came away with the idea that he had married Miss Manners. He once said she gave the best dinner parties around—how's that for passion? And I also remember him babbling about how much some partners in his law firm enjoyed her company."

"That sounds like the man we met at the wedding," Melanie told Lisa, nodding.

"Sure does," Lisa said distantly, uncomfortably. The more she heard about Gordon Noble, the more she realized she had to get to know him. And the less she liked the idea.

8

One Desperate Lady

Heckler leaned against a wall in a corner of Def-Con IV, a punk club in the Village. It was not quite midnight, so he still had room to breathe. And unwind. It was noisy, but Heckler never minded noise, and although it was crowded, it was always an interesting crowd. Heckler knew he didn't fit in completely with the knee blazers and buzz cuts around him, but he didn't particularly stand out either: before leaving the station that night he had changed back into his red leather tie, and when he went home to feed the cat, he had climbed into a pair of green camouflage pants.

Heckler had decided that afternoon that Harris Cohn was a better photographer than anyone gave him credit for, and Penny Noble was a very pretty lady. But the pictures of Noble alive depressed him more than the pictures of Noble dead, because they seemed to confirm what two Junior Leaguers and a college roommate had told him that day: the Nobles had a lousy marriage. And Penny Noble was one desperate lady. Her last hours had been spent posing for nude and seminude pictures for her husband, some in tacky new lingerie from Macy's. She had no sooner gotten dressed than someone had killed her.

One of the Junior Leaguers Heckler had interviewed, Marcia Hollensbee, had gone so far as to suggest that Gordon may actually have had something to do with Penny's murder. Although Heckler had told Marcia that Gordon certainly was a suspect, he didn't really believe that the husband was involved: the hair found at Cohn's apartment was black, while Gordon's hair was blond;

and Gordon seemed to have a perfectly good alibi for his whereabouts Wednesday night. He had worked late at the office and then gone to the University Club to play squash.

Up at the bar Heckler saw a woman alone in black tights and a man's tweed blazer. He started toward her, planning to introduce himself, when she turned to her right and he saw that she looked a bit like Penny Noble. Not a lot, but her upturned nose and the way she smiled at the bartender reminded him of the dead woman. He couldn't talk to her. Suddenly, he couldn't even stay at the club. He put down his drink on the nearest table, ignoring the glares of the couple seated there, and walked home under a starless sky.

9

Rose Petal Memories

Lisa, Melanie, and Mark left McSweet's just after midnight and piled into a cab. The cabby stopped first at Lisa's studio, where Melanie got out, and then drove back uptown to Mark's apartment. There Mark halfheartedly suggested they have a nightcap, but Lisa knew he was as tired as she was—and much drunker—and so declined.

Once in bed, Mark fell asleep quickly, folding himself around the contours of Lisa's body. She was wearing a long nightgown, partly out of modesty and partly to shield herself from his naked, sleep-driven sweat, but Mark had pulled the nightgown up above her waist and pressed himself against her rear. Sometimes the intensity Mark evidenced as he tried to conform to the shape of her body gave Lisa the feeling he was trying to crawl back into her. Other times, his pressure gave her the exact opposite impression: he was not seeking protection, but giving it, using his body as a shield. Or at least a quilt.

She was surprised that she had not thought of Leslie Nichols more seriously earlier in the day. So many of her memories of Penny involved the man, memories from both during and after college. Hadn't he once tried to get back together with Penny a year or two after she left Crosby? And hadn't Penny rejected him mercilessly?

She also remembered the sociology course of his that Penny had insisted she take their sophomore spring, "The Urban Mystique." In it they had read novels and essays written by "urban" men and women, and then discussed why, literally, a man's life was mean, nasty, brutish, and short. While there was no theme to the course, a continuing focus had been the interaction of male power and intimidation. Leslie had told the class a story during the first seminar. Stripped to its bare bones, the story was that Leslie had been walking down a Manhattan street late one evening, and was absolutely alone except for a woman walking about twenty feet ahead of him. He knew that his presence disturbed the woman and probably frightened her. To make sure she heard him approaching, he scraped his feet. When he caught up to her, he spun around to see her face. Leslie had told the class she was the most miserable woman he had ever seen. Expecting to find what he called the face of fear, he had found instead resignation, a woman older than her years who was scared of nothing, especially not men. Lisa had assumed Leslie's point was that he—yes, even Professor Touchy-Feely with his profoundly egalitarian soul—was thrilled, fascinated, and sexually excited by the power he had expected to have over this faceless woman. The point, in short, was that men were creeps.

Lisa had believed it at the time, and was relatively sure that Penny had too. Leslie, of course, was the exception. He was different. Melanie had been right in the restaurant when she had implied that all four women had

had a crush on Leslie at one time or another. Neither Lisa nor Melanie nor Christine had worshipped the man the way Penny had, but they all had found him enormously appealing.

As she lay in bed staring at the walls, she saw Penny. The thick, brown frames of the sunglasses she occasionally wore were formed by two competing circles of plaster, and the lampshade on Mark's desk looked vaguely like the hat Penny had worn when she left her wedding reception.

Was it possible, she wondered, that Penny's wedding was the last time she had seen Penny and Gordon together? She could not recall any time more recent. But she could remember them getting into a limousine together after their reception, being covered by the rose petals she and Melanie were tossing from the steps of the Colony Club. Penny was alternately laughing and crying, depending on whom she was facing: when she saw her mother waving from the top of the steps, she had cried; when she saw Lisa and Melanie, both almost helplessly drunk, she had smiled.

Remembering Penny's tears, Lisa herself began again to cry. Suddenly she wasn't so sure she wanted to write an article about Penny, and she wasn't so sure she could; suddenly, for the first time that day, she wasn't even sure that she wanted to know everything there was to know about her friend's death.

III

Friday

10

A Caring, Gentle Deviant

"There's very little clinically supervised research that definitively links secondary cigarette smoke and heart disease or secondary cigarette smoke and cancer," the man on the radio was saying.

The digital clock read 5:29, meaning in reality it was 5:24. Mark kept all his clocks five minutes fast, part of his futile strategy to get places on time. Lisa realized that he must have set the clock radio to explode at 5:29 instead of 6:29 by mistake, before passing out less than five hours earlier.

"Are you saying, Doctor, that the surgeon general is wrong?" the talk show host asked his guest.

"What I'm saying is that there is very little clinically supervised research that shows a definitive correlation between secondary cigarette smoke and either heart disease or cancer. That's what I'm saying."

Lisa reached over Mark, resting her weight on her right hand, and tapped the radio's power button with her left.

"We have time for one more call. You're on the—," the host said before dying abruptly.

"Thank you," Mark mumbled.

Lisa looked down and saw that his eyes were closed.

"You're awake," she said.

"Because I'm being punished."

"You're hung over?"

"I'm still half-drunk. And hung over."

"Let me get you something. What's in your medicine chest?"

"Pills. Capsules. Condoms."

"I'll get you aspirin."

"There are live plankton on my teeth."

"Aspirin kills plankton."

"I have a brain tumor."

"Aspirin kills tumors."

"I'm afraid to open my eyes."

"Aspirin opens people's eyes."

It was still dark outside when she got out of bed. This was the second time in a row that she had woken up and discovered it was dark outside. It reminded her of an old "Twilight Zone" episode in which the sun never rose.

The light in Mark's bathroom momentarily blinded her. She opened one eye at a time, squinting until she found a black-and-white label on the top shelf. Aspirin was the only generic bottle in the cabinet. It was a clear plastic flask surrounded by bright yellow, red, and blue boxes, bottles, and sprays. She turned each one around so that they all faced forward.

She poured three aspirin into her hand and took one herself. She rinsed the dried toothpaste out of the coffee mug beside the sink before filling it and returning to Mark. When she turned off the bathroom light, she found she was again blind, this time because of the darkness.

"You buy generic aspirin," she said, standing beside the bed.

"I know."

"It's the only generic product in there."

"I'd buy generic Contac if they made it. Or generic Robitussin. Or generic Crest."

"Those are brands. Not products. You can't have a generic brand."

Mark sat up in bed to take the aspirin. "Thank you," he said, alluding to the pills in his hand.

"You're welcome."

"Are you coming back to bed?"

"I'm not sleepy."

"It's five thirty-six in the morning."

"Five thirty-one."

"It's early."

"I guess it was the nap I took yesterday," she said, suddenly realizing that they had been speaking in soft, hushed tones. "I just don't think I can sleep."

He swung his legs over the side of the bed and pulled Lisa to him. He sat her on one of his legs and wrapped his arms around her stomach, pressing his head against her breasts. Even through her nightgown, she could feel his stubble.

"When the radio first went off," she said sadly, "I didn't remember Penny was dead. Something was wrong, but I didn't know what."

He bounced her on his knee as if she were a small child.

"It was when I came out of the bathroom that it all came back to me. The newspaper stories. The photos. The headlines. It scares me that Penny is dead. I had hardly thought about her since she got married, but now I'm afraid I won't be able to stop thinking of her."

"Sure you will. It's natural to forget about people once they die. I see it all the time," Mark said, his breath smelling like rotted clams. "It's a defense mechanism of sorts, so we don't grieve forever."

Lisa stood up and walked to the window. She jumped slightly when she was greeted by a series of steady, ear-splitting squeals: the toots required of New York City garbage trucks in reverse. "That makes me feel really super," she said. "The idea that soon I'll forget Penny. The idea that when I die, I'll be forgotten too. Super."

"Forgotten is the wrong word. All I meant is that we don't remain obsessed with the dead forever."

"Penny Noble was one of my best friends."

"The key word is 'was.'"

"She was an important person to me."

"Look, Lisa, all I'm saying is you're going to lose people along the way. Accept that. People die."

"I think I'm 'accepting' it just fine. But I'm allowed to be sad, aren't I?"

"Of course you are," he said, sounding testy. "But what's this 'important person' crap? You sound like Melanie Simple Mind."

"That's not fair, and you know it. Part of Melanie's goodness is her simplicity. Her ingenuousness."

"Ingenuous? Melanie is more affected than the makeup consultants at Bloomingdale's."

She stood in front of the window looking at him, suddenly repulsed. The roll of flab across his midsection was exaggerated by his slouch. His head was buried in his hands, making it appear as if he were contemplating his penis. By the way he glistened, she could almost feel the sweat on his skin and the sheen in his thick black hair. She wondered why, on occasion, she found him attractive.

"I don't think I can fall back to sleep," she said again. "I think I'm going to make myself some coffee."

"Fine," he said, unmoving.

In the kitchen she discovered Mark was out of Maxwell House. He had a pound of fresh Mocha Java beans beside the Braun coffee grinder, but she could not bring herself to use the machine: although she was annoyed with Mark, subjecting him to the grinder's loud, malevolent growl as it reduced the beans to coarse brown flakes would mean subjecting herself to the noise as well. It wasn't worth it. So instead she boiled water and rooted through his cabinets until she found the Red Zinger tea bags.

As she sipped her tea, relaxing, it occurred to her

that her anger was unreasonable. She would not forget Penny, but she would forget the sadness she was feeling. Mark was right: people don't remember what sadness feels like once it's gone. Moreover, there really was no reason she should expect Mark to understand her friendship with Melanie. Or her friendship with Christine or Penny. Their friendship wasn't important to them the way it once was.

Still, although she knew her annoyance was irrational, it wouldn't go away. Mark could have shown more tenderness, more concern. He should have been more tolerant. But what kind of sensitivity could she expect from a man who left his shaving stubble in the sink each morning, sometimes beside her toothbrush? Who sweated in his sleep? Who kept his tea bags in a half-filled cardboard canister of Quaker Oats? There may have been as many sloppy women in the world as there were sloppy men, but few as unhygienic or disordered. Male dirt and disorder were probably the greatest historical causes of lesbianism. Greater certainly than male oppression, female narcissism, and husbands who hate cunnilingus.

Lisa was startled when the phone rang, two rapid uneven chirps, just after 6:00 A.M. She immediately looked toward the refrigerator, assuming that because her phone was beside her refrigerator Mark's phone was beside his, but after a second she remembered that his telephone was on the floor beside a driftwood sculpture of Haitian rats. She reached it on the third ring, but whoever was calling hung up immediately after Lisa said hello.

Mark staggered into the living room wearing a pair of baggy khakis, either woken by the telephone or at least dragged out of bed by it. He saw that Lisa had already returned the receiver to its cradle.

"Who was that?" he asked, rubbing his eyes with his fists.

"I don't know."

"You don't know?"

"No. They hung up." She wondered at her choice of pronoun. They. Was it to avoid any presumption of the caller's gender? Or was it a latent fear of conspiracies, acknowledging the possibility that a group of burglars, rapists, or psychotics was casing the apartment? Or simply tormenting its occupants?

Mark sat down on the couch, flopping himself on to its cushions like he was just one more of the fat throw pillows at either end.

"Why did I piss you off?" he asked. The question betrayed no anxiety, no vulnerability, no frenzied fear of possible answers. It was asked with the same sleepy casualness he evidenced when he had asked her who called a moment earlier.

"You didn't 'piss me off,'" she said, lying because the question surprised her. She had not expected to have an earnest discussion of their relationship at this hour.

"Okay. What did I do to irritate you?" he continued.

"You were mean to me."

"When?"

He knew exactly when. Lisa was sure of it. He knew what he had done, and he probably knew he was wrong; but before he apologized, he would make her swallow some pride and spell out exactly why she was hurt.

"A few minutes ago."

"Rocking you on my knees is mean?"

"Forget it," she said, returning to the kitchen to get her tea.

He was silent for a moment, undoubtedly because to continue the discussion while she was in the kitchen would mean raising his voice. She had learned that his favorite tactic was to remain calm, to keep his voice serene, even, almost paternal. It could be maddening. When she returned to the living room with her tea, he was concentrating on a long black hair on his upper arm. Seeing her, he looked up and said, "Seriously, Lisa, help me with this. What have I done to tick you off?"

"I told you. You were mean to me."

"How? I want to know."

She sat down by the drop-leaf table and stared at an 1858 daguerreotype of a brass factory in Waterbury, Connecticut. There were orange crucifixes painted above the three smoking chimneys.

"I think," she said, trying to sound as calm as Mark, "that your assessment of my friends was cruel."

"I didn't mean to be cruel."

"And you snapped at me."

"I didn't mean to snap at you. That I know."

"You did."

"I didn't. At least I didn't mean to."

"You snapped when you said Penny and I weren't friends. You snapped when you said Melanie was as superficial as a Bloomingdale's makeup consultant. That was cruel."

He smiled. "I think that was pretty clever, considering it came from someone dying at five-thirty in the morning."

"That's what I mean!" she cried out, astounded that he had given her a ready example of his callousness. "A friend of mine is murdered, and listen to you. Listen to you! You tell me I'll forget her. You tell me Melanie is superficial. You tell me my grief is superficial," she said, her voice cracking.

"I didn't mean to," he said, looking away.

"But you did!"

"Look, I didn't mean to. If you think I did, I'm sorry," he said, rising and going to her. He squatted before her, his hands on her knees. "I felt awful, I was half-asleep. Maybe I wasn't thinking. But I'm sorry. I know this is a tough time for you, and I don't want to fight."

She didn't want to accept his apology. Her anger seemed juvenile to her, his apology condescending. But to ignore him, tell him it was too late, do anything other than accept it would make her the aggressor. Their fight would become her fault, a responsibility she neither wanted nor believed she deserved. She coasted forward until her forehead hit his shoulder, and rested there. The action tacitly signaled a truce.

"I really am sorry."

She nodded against his shoulder.

"Want more tea?"

"No." Staring straight down she saw a small dried orange spot on his khakis. Tomato sauce, maybe strawberry something. She sat up, so he stood up.

"Well, I'm going to make some coffee. I don't think I'll go back to bed either. I'd be getting up in another twenty minutes anyway."

He went to the kitchen, and she listened as he discovered he would have to grind beans if he wanted coffee. She heard him put the kettle on the stove, meaning he, too, had decided the coffee wasn't worth the effort.

"Are we doing anything tonight with Melanie and Christine?" Mark asked, returning to the table with his tea.

"I don't know. It will depend on them. I don't think we'll do much."

"Just let me know." He sipped his tea, staring down at the tea bag floating on the amber surface. Abruptly he looked up, smiling. "We're friends again, right?"

"We never stopped."

"Good. What do you say I grab a shower and a shave so I don't look like I belong on Riker's Island, and then meet you in the bedroom in ten minutes? If we're going to be up at this hour, we might as well use the time productively, and violate some blue laws."

He astounded her. A half-hour earlier he could barely move, and now he wanted to have sex. He was like a little boy. "It will take more than ten minutes to shave off that convict's stubble," she said.

"Fifteen, then."

"Try a day. It will take electrolysis."

"So be it. Shall we?"

"God, you're persistent."

"Obsessed."

"Try deviant."

"But a caring, sensitive deviant. A gentle deviant. A deviant concerned with the needs and wants of his partner. A deviant who knows about g-spots, g-strings, and Jacuzzis."

"How can you think of sex now?"

"I'm awake."

"Stay with me while I finish my tea. Then we'll take a bath and see what happens."

"How about a tongue bath?"

"Find a cat."

"A bubble bath?"

"I don't promise deviants anything," she said, reaching under the table and squeezing his erection through his khakis.

11

Glimmer, Bloom, and Rival

Lisa had never had a whole lot of respect for Warren Racine, but his refusal to give her the list of Dayton-Patterson product managers confirmed in her mind once and for all that the man was a certifiable creep. A certifiable creep with a spine made of Jell-O. It wasn't a difficult task to get the names of Penny's associates at D-P, but it annoyed her that it took any work at all.

As soon as she got into the office Friday morning, she called Charlie Barrows in media. And then Ronnie Thompson. And then Maria Ridalgo. Three phone calls to the three media planners on the D-P account, the people who decided whether Whisper should advertise on

"As the World Turns" or "L.A. Law," or whether Lore should buy space in *Vanity Fair* or *Ladies' Home Journal*. From them, Lisa got the names of Penny's fellow product managers on Glimmer Shampoo, Bloom Deodorant, and Rival Detergent. Along with Whisper, they represented D-P's flagship brands, some—like Rival—going back eighty years.

When she had the names in front of her on one piece of paper, she tried to decide who had the nicest name, and who based on name alone would be most willing to talk to her. It was a stupid strategy, Lisa knew, but no stupider than tossing coins to decide who to call first. When she was through, she phoned Dayton-Patterson and asked to speak with Melissa Hayes.

"Melissa Hayes's office, this is Tina," a young woman answered. Lisa thought that the secretary sounded about seventeen.

"Hi, this is Lisa Stone at O-M-R. Is Melissa there?"

"Just a minute, please, let me check," Tina said.

Lisa was put on hold for only a very few seconds. Evidently, Melissa had no qualms about speaking with Lisa, even though she had no idea who Lisa was.

"Good morning, this is Melissa Hayes," the D-P executive said, greeting Lisa with more cheer than Lisa thought necessary. Still, it was a very nice, professional voice.

"How do you do, Melissa? My name is Lisa Stone. I work with Warren Racine in account management at O-M-R."

"Ah, Warren. Voted ad man most likely to make the cover of *GQ*," Melissa said, snickering.

"I'm glad to hear that D-P appreciates his bow ties as much as we do."

"Absolutely! Especially the one with the owls."

"That's from his days on Wise Potato Chips, you know."

"Is that true?"

63

"Sure is. It was a gift from the brand managers on Wise."

Melissa made a clicking sound into the phone with her tongue, a tsk. "And to think the only thing we give him is a hard time."

"Oh, I don't know about that. I think he loves the business."

"You ad people stick together, don't you?"

"We have to. It's a small community," Lisa said. She decided she liked Melissa.

"So what can I do for you?" Melissa asked after a short pause.

"I'm calling about a friend."

"Who wants a job in marketing, right? Sure, I'll talk to 'em."

"I don't think that's possible."

"No?"

"No. This friend is dead," Lisa said evenly. The word was every bit as hard to say as she expected. Maybe even harder.

"You're calling about Penny Noble, aren't you?"

"That's right."

"Why?"

"She was my friend. We went to school together."

"So what do you want from me? You were probably a lot closer to her than I was."

"Probably. But evidently, I didn't know her as well as I thought. That's why I was hoping you could go to lunch with me. I want to talk a little about the Penny I knew, and hear about the Penny you knew. I may even try and write an article about this whole mess."

"I don't think I have the time," Melissa answered, suddenly curt.

"How about a drink then?"

"No. We have our annual sales meeting coming up in two weeks, and I need to prepare for it. I have no time at all."

"Can I call you in a couple weeks then? When your calendar has opened up a bit."

"You can, yes, but I doubt I'll have the time to see you then either. I'm sorry, but I was just on my way to a meeting when you called. I have to run. It was nice talking to you."

"Thanks anyway," Lisa said, but Melissa already had hung up.

She sat back in her chair, more perplexed than angry. Melissa had said she had the time to talk to a stranger about a job, but she couldn't spare twenty minutes to talk about Penny Noble. She wondered whether it was the idea of the article that had caused Melissa to clam up, or whether Melissa would have clammed up in any case. She made a mental note that she wouldn't mention the article when she called her other D-P leads. She also realized she had better call those leads that very moment: it suddenly seemed important to reach them before Melissa did.

Immediately she phoned Ben Bergen, the senior product manager on Rival. Bergen, however, was not in his office, so all Lisa could do was leave a message for him to call. She then asked Bergen's secretary to transfer her to Walt Swaggert on Bloom.

"Hello?" a gruff, older voice answered. Lisa envisioned a heavyset man in a short-sleeved business shirt.

"Hello, is this Walter Swaggert?"

"Last time I checked, it was. Who's this?"

"You don't know me. My name is Lisa Stone. I'm an account executive at O-M-R."

"I'm happy for you."

"I was hoping you could help me."

Swaggert made a noise somewhere between a snort and a chuckle. "What do you need? Neilsen shares? SAMI shares? Sales in drug stores? Sales in supermarkets? Sales by size, by unit, by case? I got more numbers than hair."

"Actually, I was hoping to talk about a friend of mine. Penny Noble."

"Jeez, that's a sad one, isn't it? I'm sorry for you, Lisa, I really am. She was a helluva gal."

"She was. We went to school together."

"The thing I always liked about her was the fact she was responsible. I'd ask her to do something once, and I'd know it would get done. And get done right. Unlike a lot of those young MBA prima donnas, Penny was a good worker."

"She worked for you?"

Swaggert laughed. "I was her first boss here! I broke her in. She was my assistant for almost a year on Sunshine. We've both moved on since, but we worked together back then."

"Really?"

"Really."

"Well, I'd like to talk about her with someone else who knew her. So I was hoping you might be able to have lunch with me one day early next week."

"Oh, you forward young woman. Sure, I'd be happy to. Penny was a real star, I thought. Could you hold on a second, someone just came in my office."

Lisa was so excited that she nearly clapped her hands together. Quickly she scanned her appointment book to see if Monday or Tuesday was free. She already had a lunch date on Monday, but it was the sort of thing she could move if Swaggert were available.

A moment later Swaggert came back on the phone. "Lisa? It's Lisa, right?"

"Right. Lisa Stone. How is Monday, Walter?"

"Rotten. Monday is going to be real bad. Fact is, all of next week is going to be a bear. Looking at my to-do lists, I don't think I'll have a free minute all next week."

Lisa took a deep breath, and tried not to panic. "How about a drink after work in that case?"

"It would be midnight, Lisa, midnight. I'll be pushing papers into the wee hours of the A.M. next week. You see, we have a big-deal annual sales meeting in two weeks, and—"

"Did Melissa Hayes just talk to you?" The question had more of an edge to it than Lisa wanted. But she was angry, and the question—accusation, really—just exploded from her lips.

"Why do you ask?"

"Because not one minute ago we were going to have lunch. Then someone came into your office, you put me on hold, and the next thing I know you won't see me."

"I never said I wouldn't see you. Don't you think you're getting a little paranoid there?"

"Okay, if you'll see me, let's set a date."

"Now look here. Getting riled up and bitched off is no way to coax me into breaking bread with you. Be smart."

"I'm sorry, Walter. But I'm upset about Penny's death."

"We all are. I promise you, we all are."

"So can we get together and talk about her?"

"I'll call you next week, Lisa, and we'll see about setting something up for later in the month. How would that be?"

"Is that the best I'm going to get?"

"That's the best. Swaggert's best."

"Okay, fine. I'll talk to you next week."

"Good enough. Nice talking to you," Swaggert said before hanging up.

Lisa returned the receiver to the cradle, frustrated. She knew Swaggert wouldn't call her. She knew Bergen wouldn't call her. Melissa Hayes would make sure of that.

12

"The Safest Sex There Is . . ."

It figured, Heckler thought to himself, it figured. If anyone was going to have a kid brother working selling sex toys, it would be Harris Cohn.

Rudy Cohn was a tall, slim man in his mid twenties who was still fighting an adolescent's battle with acne. A losing battle. Heckler found him a little before lunch behind the checkout counter of the Guys and Dolls Boutique—a corridor, essentially, between two Forty-second Street peep show parlors. The younger Cohn had been busted twice before, once for possession of a deadly weapon (a loaded derringer) and once for drug possession (cocaine). The weapons rap, his first offense, had landed him three years probation and one hundred hours of community service; the drug charges had been dropped on a technicality.

Heckler had no desire to talk to Rudy Cohn, and no faith at all that Cohn would be able to help him, but he also knew that if he didn't spend some time checking out Harris Cohn's friends and family, he wouldn't be able to live with himself. His whole investigation would be suspect in his mind.

"You're Rudy Cohn, right?" Heckler asked as he approached the counter. There were two other men in the back of the store pawing over triple-X videocassettes.

"Yeah. Who are you?"

Heckler flashed his badge briefly. "Richard Heckler, Homicide. I'm here to talk about your brother."

Cohn curled his lip defiantly. "What about him?"

"Well, first of all, I want you to know I'm sorry. And I understand this is a tough time for you—"

"Life is tough," Cohn said, cutting him off.

Heckler paused, noting that Rudy Cohn had no need for condolences. "It is," he said after a moment, "it is. So tell me, do you know anything about your brother's death?"

"Zip."

"Do you know anything about your brother's business?"

"Zero."

"Do you know anything about your brother's photography?"

"Nada."

One of the men from the back, a middle-aged businessman in a gray overcoat, joined Cohn and Heckler at the counter. He was buying two videocassettes, *The Sperminator* and *Vannah and Her Sisters*. He paid cash and wouldn't look either Cohn or Heckler in the eye.

When the businessman had left, Heckler said calmly, "Rudy, I can make your life worth less than shit. I have a feeling this place here is just crying to be shut down for a couple of days. Maybe searched. Maybe searched thoroughly."

"You got nothing on me."

"I wouldn't need anything. I can make your life worth less than shit with zip. Zero. Or nada."

Cohn looked down at the counter and shrugged. "I don't know what you want from me."

"Some answers. Some real simple answers. I'll get real specific for you, make it real easy."

"Don't be talking down to me."

"It's the only way I can talk to the gutter, Rudy."

Cohn continued to stare down at the glass counter. When he didn't look up, Heckler continued, "So tell me, do you know if Harris had any enemies?"

"I don't think so. If he did, he never told me."

"Was his murder drug-related?"

"What do you mean?"

"Did someone kill him because they wanted drugs? Or because he had sold them some bad shit?"

"Harris didn't sell drugs."

"That's bullshit, Rudy, and you know it. We found enough junk in his closet to clean up Columbia's debt with the World Bank," Heckler told him, lying.

"Maybe you did. But if Harris was dealin', he didn't deal on the street, or to the kind of person who carries a piece."

"What kind of person did he sell to, in that case?"

"I never said he sold anything."

"I understand, Rudy. We're talking theory."

"Right."

"Who would Harris sell to if he sold at all, which you're not saying he did."

"Rich people. Those rich weirdos he used to take pictures of. And their friends, I guess."

"Harris used to take pictures of a lot of rich people, huh?"

Cohn reached behind the counter and pulled out copies of the *Village Voice* and *New York* magazine. In each issue he turned to the classified section and pointed out the identical five-line ad in both:

NUDE PORTRAITURE: Tasteful, erotic portraits done—for portfolio, for gifts, for yourself. Nude and seminude. Always refined, elegant, and artistic. And *always* confidential. Call 555-3434.

When he had finished reading the ad, Heckler looked up, asking, "Harris made his entire living this way?"

"That surprises you?"

"Well, yes. It does. I can't believe he had that big a clientele."

"He didn't need a big one. Three hundred bucks a sitting. Twenty bucks a print. And two hundred bucks for the negatives—sometimes more. And he said he used to do two or three girls a week."

"Girls?"

"Women. You know I mean women. Nice clean ladies from like Greenwich Village, and Park Avenue, and Connecticut."

"And you think Harris might have sold those nice clean ladies drugs."

Rudy Cohn slammed his hand down hard on the counter top. "No! I didn't say that. All I said is if anybody dealt any shit—and I said if—it would have had to have been to them. Harris was no street hustler!"

"So who killed him? Could it have been the husband of a nice clean lady from Connecticut?"

"Coulda been."

A couple in their mid thirties, out-of-towners, Heckler surmised, wandered into the store and up to Rudy. Heckler saw no reason to ruin one of Rudy's sales, so he backed away from the counter and began strolling around the store. He was fascinated. He saw blow-up dolls with gyro-powered love openings, lactating rubber tits, rubber pants, rubber gloves, leather masks, crotchless panties, bras with nibble-nipple holes, stay-hard creams, jellies, foams, and powders, diaphragm frisbees, Jell-O Wrestling, Parkay Twister, water pistol penises, penis pens, penis puppets, penis pipes, and the more conventional Swedish erotica—dirty books, movies, cassettes, and playing cards. Above a row of vibrators—white ones, black ones, blue ones, clear ones, ribbed ones, ones that were anatomically accurate—was a handwritten sign that read, THE SAFEST SEX THERE IS, IS YOUR OWN SEX TOY!

When Heckler turned around, the other couple had left. "So Rudy, you make the sale?" he asked.

"You mean to the two feebs who were just here?"

"Right. To the two feebs."

"Nah. They thought they'd get AIDS just from touching the stuff."

"Could they?"

Rudy folded his arms across his chest and smiled. "I wouldn't worry, detective. It takes a lot more than eye-balling the stuff to get the slims. If you got it, you didn't get it here."

Heckler nodded, thanked Rudy, and left. He reminded himself that he had to wash his hands the first chance he got.

13

"Big Ol' Skeleton"

Lisa didn't work closely enough with Jack O'Donnell to view him as a mentor, but she knew he looked out for her. Protected her. Lisa was fairly sure that it was O'Donnell who had engineered her move on to Pilgrim Paper, and who had then seen to it that she was promoted twice in only eighteen months.

O'Donnell was an O-M-R career man, in some ways the classic O-M-R executive: early fifties, a full head of thick gray hair, immaculately tailored suits from Barney's, a squash game that devastated men half his age on a weekly basis. He was the account director on Dayton-Patterson, Pilgrim, and the agency's beer account, making him one of the two or three most powerful men in the New York office.

Lisa rarely spoke to him outside of elevators and the quarterly brand reviews, so she was surprised when he dropped by her office late morning. She was on her way out to lunch with Melanie and Christine when he knocked on her open door.

"Jack, hello," she said, trying to sound casual.

"What brings you to this neck of the woods?" He was irritated, she could tell by his posture: he was standing perfectly straight, his hands clasped behind his back.

"I hear you're working on D-P now," he said, forcing a smile.

"Really? Do you know something I don't?" she answered, joking.

"No. I don't think so. But I just got off the phone with Ed Simmonds, vice president of marketing at D-P, and he tells me you've been on the phone all morning with his brand managers."

"That's a bit of an exaggeration. I spoke to a couple of them for a grand total of ten minutes, that's all."

"Why?"

"Why did I call them?"

"Yes. Why is my senior account executive on Pilgrim Paper phoning brand managers at Dayton-Patterson?"

Lisa sat back against the edge of her desk, giving herself a moment to calm down and think through her answers. "The D-P woman who was killed Wednesday night was one of my college roommates. We had been good friends once."

"I'm sorry. That must have been a real shock," O'Donnell said, softening a bit.

Lisa nodded. "Oh yeah," she said, "it sure was. It sure is. I'm still in shock."

"Can I make a suggestion?"

"Sure."

"Why don't you take the rest of the day off? Go home, take it easy. Begin the weekend an afternoon early."

"I went home early yesterday."

"So?"

"Do I look that bad? Do I look like I need to go home?"

"No, of course not."

"Then I'll come back after lunch. I have a lot of work to do."

"Your decision. Just do me one favor. Do yourself one favor. Don't call D-P anymore."

"Oh come on, Jack. Give me some credit. I don't know what Simmonds told you, but I wasn't harassing anyone over there. You must know me well enough to know that."

"It's not what you say, it's what they hear. Advertising rule number nine. Or ten, maybe. Whatever. The point is, two D-P brand managers told Simmonds you were calling all morning and hinting D-P had something to do with this Noble woman's death."

"That's just not true," Lisa said, raising her voice.

"But that's what they heard."

"They heard wrong! I never said anything like that!"

"That's fine, and I believe you. But it doesn't matter. You can't call D-P anymore. I'm sorry, but that company is now off limits. Understand?"

Furious, Lisa was unable to look at O'Donnell. He sounded like he thought he was her father. "I understand," she said, staring down at his shoes. "But it doesn't make sense."

It was a cool spring day, the air smelling like rain. As Lisa left the O-M-R building and began attempting to merge with the streams of harried lunch-hour executives, she froze momentarily on the sidewalk. Despite the crowd and the uninterrupted waves of movement, she began to experience the same nervous loneliness she used to feel when she would cross the deserted Crosby campus late at night. A vulnerability of sorts. Although she had lived in Manhattan for six years, this was the first time she had felt it in the city. She knew the sensation was unfounded, but she was sure she was being watched. She scanned the people across the street. Two women talking by the awning of the croissant shop, one weighted down by a black and red Saks bag. She saw a young man barely out of college with a crisp new attaché case, strutting toward a parked cab. She saw the corner's street psycho, a Vietnam veteran who played a ukulele and hissed. It was harmless, everyone was harmless. Yet she began to walk a little faster than she normally did.

She had told Christine and Melanie that she would meet them at a restaurant near her Gramercy Park apartment, a wine and cheese place called the Wine Rack, so she headed over to the Fifty-first Street subway stop. When she thought about lunch and about seeing Christine, her uneasiness momentarily faded. As she stood on the subway platform, however, the sensation returned. Every story she had ever heard or had seen in the tabloids of women being pushed under oncoming subways by unknown, unfound, unprosecuted strangers came back to her. Instead of waiting for the train by the yellow line at the edge of the tracks, she stood a good three yards from the edge, her back touching the tile wall. When the subway arrived, thundering into the station, she looked guardedly around her, but no one was within ten feet. When she entered the car, she stood beside the door, although there were plenty of empty seats. She wanted to be able to run to another car if—if she wanted to.

When she exited the subway at Twenty-third Street, she ran up the steps two at a time. No one was following her. She whispered to herself that she was a big baby and forced herself to smile, concentrating on the physical movement of turning up the sides of her mouth.

When she reached the restaurant, she saw that Christine and Melanie had already arrived. They were sitting on opposite sides of the table, facing each other like angry diplomats. When Christine saw Lisa, she stood up and met Lisa midway between the restaurant's entrance and her table, wrapping her ample arms around her in a bear hug.

Lisa's first thought was that Christine was still every bit as heavy as she had feared; the woman certainly didn't need lunch in a place that specialized in beer and cheese fondue.

"You look good," Christine whispered to Lisa.

"It's good to see you," Lisa said, patting Christine on the back. She was disconcerted by the flecks of gray beginning to emerge in Christine's frizzy black halo, and how poorly Christine was dressed. It looked as if Christine had given up on her appearance and now wore the most second-rate things she could find: brown corduroys and a ratty red sweater that didn't match. Melanie, as always, was distinctively more stylish, wearing leather slacks and a tight-fitting long-sleeved Hard Rock Café T-shirt.

As the pair separated, Melanie picked up the hanging strand of their conversation, telling Christine, "I just don't understand why you stay. It must be awfully awkward."

"Give me some credit, will you?" Christine hissed at her old roommate, her anger returning almost immediately. "Of course it's awkward. But what in the name of Sam Hill am I supposed to say to Gordon? 'Oh, gee, Gordon, so sorry Penny's dead. I better go to a hotel now because you're just too weird to be around.' How does that sound, Mel? You like the ring of it?"

For a brief moment Lisa watched Melanie and Christine. For two people rumored to be friends, they always seemed to be fighting. Except when Penny had been around. They didn't scratch at each other like this when Penny was with them.

"Slow down," Lisa said, hoping with her interruption to calm her friends down. "I'm coming in in the middle. Let me get a glass of wine, and then let's order. And then you can argue."

"We weren't arguing," Melanie said, after they had ordered a cauldron of fondue. "I just told Christine that I can't imagine staying in Gordon and Penny's apartment now that Penny is gone. We—Christine especially— hardly knew Gordon."

"It's just not a big deal," Christine insisted. "One, I

don't want to hurt the guy's feelings. Two, I'm helpin' out a bit. I'm a whiz at shit-cannin' reporters."

"They're calling Gordon a lot, huh?" Lisa asked.

"You can bet your sweet fanny, they are. My favorite is Charlotte Gruper of the *New York Post*. I love shit-cannin' her. Big ol' redhead Amazon gal. Just a peach to hang up on."

"Do you think it would be okay if I called Gordon this afternoon?"

"Don't see why not. I told him you called yesterday to express your condolences."

"Well, I would also like to ask him a few questions."

"What for?" Christine asked.

"I'm going to write an article about Penny. For *New York* maybe. Something to dispute all the stuff the newspapers have been saying about a double life. I guess it will be my way of 'shit-canning' Charlotte Gruper."

Christine put a golf-ball-sized piece of bread in her mouth. "Sure, you can call the boy," she said, chewing. "But it seems pretty darn tasteless to me. And I don't think he'll tell you much you don't already know."

"Why do you say that?"

"Because you knew Penny a helluva lot better than Gordon. We all did!"

"I agree and I disagree. I knew one Penny very well. The Penny I went to Crosby with, the Penny from the Social Register, the Penny who went to work for D-P. But maybe there was a Penny I didn't know. I didn't know Penny the wife at all. I don't have a clue why Penny was with that Harris Cohn fellow."

"I can answer that one for you," Christine said, rolling her eyes. "I think I can shed some light on both those questions."

"I'm all ears," Lisa said.

"It's Monday night, see," Christine began, lowering her voice melodramatically. "I've been in town one day, one day mind you. Gordon is workin' late, so we've been catching up on old times, shootin' the shit. Penny's tellin' me about her big deal, hot-shit job, what a star she is, how life is all cream pies and daffodils. I tell her about my asinine job, how life is all sucking down rotten eggs. You know, one of our typical exchanges.

"Well, at one point, Penny lets me in on this big ol' skeleton in her closet. Or what she thinks is a skeleton. She and Gordon, she says, have a rotten marriage. Been married a whoopin' six months, and already she's regrettin' it big time."

"Gordon is so handsome," Melanie said softly. "How could they have had a bad marriage?"

"No spark," Christine said, spitting out the s for emphasis. "Gordon is a nice guy, I guess, but he's not real passionate. I'm not sure what was holdin' that marriage together, but it sure wasn't the bedroom."

"That's her skeleton?" Lisa asked. "That's it?"

"Yup. But it gets more interesting, trust me. Wednesday night, see, she was gonna do something about it. She knows this guy, she says, down in Greenwich Village. A photographer who'll do nude stuff. Not really an artist, but not pond scum either. Her big idea is to have him take nudie pictures of her that she can give to Gordon. To sorta recharge his batteries, I guess. Get him interested in a husbandly sort of way."

"And that photographer was Harris Cohn?"

"You bet. And you wanna hear the most awful part?" Christine continued. "The most awful part is that I mighta saved her life if I wasn't so damn pathetic."

Lisa sat back in her chair. "How?"

"I went shoppin' with Penny Wednesday afternoon, after work. To pick out her wardrobe for the pictures. Lingerie, frilly stuff. This was gonna be a real big production, you see. And I was supposed to go with her to this Cohn guy's studio. Serve like the female nurse in a male gynecologist's office, I guess.

"But at the last minute, I chickened out. I just didn't wanna have anything to do with the whole shebang. It was too damn creepy. So at the last minute, when we were done shoppin', I told her she was on her own. I told her I didn't want anything to do with her photographs. And then I went back to her apartment."

"Oh God, Christine, you could have been killed too!" Melanie gasped.

"Well, that's one way of lookin' at it. The other way is Penny might still be alive."

"What did the police say about all this?" Lisa asked.

Christine sat forward against the table and stared into Lisa's eyes. "Listen real good to this, Lis, listen real good. I only told the police that Penny and me went shoppin' for underwear. I told them I left Penny alone at Herald Square because my feet hurt, not because she was doin' something stupid. I did not tell them I knew why Penny went to Harris Cohn's. I did not tell them I knew anything about Harris Cohn's. Hell, I wouldn't have told 'em about the underwear, except there were so many people who saw us."

"I don't get it, Christine," Lisa said, staring back. "Why didn't you tell them everything?"

"Because Penny was my friend. I was trying to protect her and her family."

"But everyone knows she was with Harris Cohn."

"But everyone might not know why she was there. Wednesday night when the police called and Gordon and me went down to the station, I learned that Penny was found with all her clothes on. It's possible she was killed before the session, see? And if that's the case, then it's possible no one will ever have to know she was going to have those nudie pictures done. Or that she and Gordon had a lousy marriage."

"But if she was killed after her portraits were done, won't the police know you were lying?" Lisa asked.

Christine shook her head. "No way. They'd just think I didn't know anything at all about Harris Cohn. They'd just think Penny didn't tell me anything about him or her plans."

"Did Penny tell you how she knew Cohn?"

"No, as the matter of fact, she didn't," Christine said, sounding slightly perplexed.

"You never asked?"

"Hey, come on, Lis. You sound like a cop yourself."

"I'm just surprised. I would have asked."

"Well, I didn't. I was so weirded out by the whole thing, I guess that one question never had room in my little brain," Christine answered defensively.

"I really would go to a hotel, Christine," Melanie said again. "I just can't imagine it's a healthy situation to be so close to all this."

"What do you think Gordon's gonna do?"

"It's not Gordon," Melanie said, "it's you I'm talking about. I mean emotionally. All this violence, and the police, and the reporters. It can't be good for you."

"Can I ask you something else?" Lisa asked Christine.

"Sure, go ahead. I didn't mean to jump on you."

"Do you really think it's safe to be around Gordon? Could he have had something to do with Penny's death?"

"Now is this for your article? Or for you?"

"Both, I guess."

"First off, for Penny's sake, I wouldn't write down any of the stuff I've already told you. For Penny's sake. Understand?"

Lisa nodded, but it was just to appease Christine.

"Second, I wouldn't put anything past Gordon. The man is cold as trout. He says he was working late and then playing squash Wednesday night, but all I know is he wasn't home. Still, I don't really believe he's capable of killin' someone. Especially Penny."

"No?"

"No."

"Let me bounce one more thought off you. Last night, Melanie and I were telling Mark about Crosby and Penny and living together. Leslie Nichols came up. So I got to thinking: could Leslie Nichols have had something to do with Penny's death?"

Christine folded her hands on the table and looked earnestly into Lisa's eyes. "Is it a fever, girl?" she asked. "Or just drugs? Good God, I haven't thought about that oversexed piece of dirt in years. What in the world makes you think that man could have had anything to do with any of this?"

Lisa smiled wearily. "No real reason. But I have this vague memory of him trying to get back together with Penny a year or two after college, and Penny wanting no part of it. I guess it's silly, but I have him on the brain today."

"Well, I'd get him off the brain," Christine said. "As scummy as Leslie is, I don't think he takes his ruthlessness with him on the road."

"I just can't believe we're having this conversation," Melanie blurted out suddenly. She looked like she was about to cry. "Look at us! We're talking about Penny's husband killing her, we're talking about Leslie Nichols killing her! I'm hearing that Penny went out to have naked pictures taken of herself! Christine, you've lied to the police. We're all fighting, and Lisa wants to write an article about it! How did we get here?" she asked, beginning to sob. "How did we get to this?"

Oblivious to the people staring, Christine put an arm around Melanie's shoulder and hugged her. "You've always had a way of bringing us back to earth, you know that?"

Melanie nodded, and tried to smile. She wiped her eyes unself-consciously on the sleeve of her shirt.

"Let's face it," Christine went on, "life's dealt us all some pretty strange cards. If you had told me six years ago that when I was twenty-eight I'd weigh 205 pounds, sell greeting cards with orchids on them for a living, and live alone in Atlanta, I'd have said you were nuts. I was never as cute as you all, or as popular, but I still thought I was hot shit back then."

"We all did," Lisa reminded her.

"We'd get great jobs," Christine said, "we'd get a husband, a housekeeper, and make adorable blond children. Even me. I thought I'd be a vice president by now, making a hundred thousand dollars a year. Happily married, multiorgasmic. I thought I'd have a baby by twenty-eight, one that didn't drool or fuck up its diapers."

"You knew your baby would drool," Melanie said, sniffling.

"No way. Not my baby."

"Sure would. You drool," Lisa added, smiling.

"I will thank you to keep your comments 'bout my saliva to yourself, if you please."

Lisa laughed just the slightest bit. "And you know what is the most ironic thing? Out of all of us, the only one who seemed close to doing it right—good job, good husband, good home—was Penny."

"Yup," Christine nodded. "And just look what it got her."

Melanie really was better than all of them, Lisa decided as she rode the subway back to midtown. Melanie was not always as sharp, but she was more sincere, more giving, more caring. She didn't have a bad bone in her body, Lisa thought to herself, and she had never had a bad impulse.

She recalled the time she and Melanie had taken the bus together back to Crosby from Manhattan's Port Authority, the first time they had ever spent any real time together. It was after Thanksgiving recess their freshman year. Although they were not close friends at the time, they already were more than casual acquaintances. They had to be, because they were among the few freshmen in one of the largest houses on campus. But it was still just a happy coincidence that they wound up on the same bus.

Caught in an unexpectedly heavy early season snowstorm, the bus had slogged its way off the highway and into Bridgeport at about five miles an hour, unable to even reach New Haven, where Lisa had friends. While some of the passengers spent the night in the bus terminal, Lisa and Melanie agreed that although the accommodations on the bus were not as spacious as the benches in the station, they were infinitely safer. And more sanitary. The fact that one needed a ticket to board the bus actually made it an extremely exclusive little club. Only about eight people remained on the bus, all but one a student, all but two women. Sitting on their sides so they could face each other, bundled up in their down parkas and plaid scarves (Melanie was still two years away from leather bomber jackets and four from capes), Melanie and Lisa smoked Melanie's dope and talked until they fell asleep in the middle of the night. Melanie guiltily confessed to stealing a Williams senior's overcoat so he would miss the last bus back to his college and spend the night with her, and to letting an insistent junior in her house crawl into bed with her one other night, when her roommate was gone (but, she added defensively, she had not let the junior kiss her. Anywhere.). She confessed to making up her lab results in an astronomy course, because she didn't want to hurt the professor's feelings by admitting that astronomy bored her to tears, and to secretly harboring two stray cats in her room, because the temperature was already dropping below thirty degrees each night. The stories astonished Lisa, because she had nothing nearly so interesting to relate. Lisa had kissed neither man nor woman in the three months she had been at Crosby, nor had she even considered breaking any college regulations.

But Melanie herself had astonished Lisa as well because, inexplicably, Melanie seemed to be looking to her for guidance. And approval. Lisa thought it should be the other way around, that she should be impressed with the sexy, aggressive, resourceful Melanie Braverman. But instead Melanie was looking up to Lisa. Lisa had told herself that it must be because she had a reputation for being good-natured, or orderly, or reasonable, but she also understood that this was probably more self-image than public image. It might have been simply that Lisa was three inches taller than Melanie. Or, Melanie may have mistaken Lisa's freshman timidity for experienced reserve. Regardless, Melanie was drawn to Lisa, and their night in Bridgeport set the pattern for their college friendship: Melanie would look to Lisa for both guidance and support, even after she knew that while Lisa was smarter than she was, she was much less knowledgeable.

When the subway came to a stop at the Fifty-first Street station, Lisa started to exit. She stopped, however, before she left the train, remembering Melanie's question in the restaurant. How did they get there, she wondered? Why was Penny dead?

She sat back down, deciding to ride the subway another three stops to Seventy-seventh Street. Christine had mentioned that Gordon was at home that afternoon, making the final arrangements for Saturday's funeral. It was probably not a good time to talk to him, Lisa realized, but she also didn't think there would be a better one anytime soon.

14

Where Harris Hid His Stuff

At first Heckler felt embarrassed. But then he just felt drunk. He ran his fingers through silk ballerina teddies, sleepshirts in satin and lace, lustrous bikinis with satin ribbons. He glided from one section to another, from bras to panties, to camisoles, to tap pants. He slid to a stop before a lilac bustier, enamored with its Victorian array of hooks, ties, and underwire. My God, he thought to himself, giddy, women actually wear this stuff.

An older, blue-haired saleswoman abruptly interrupted his reverie, asking him if he needed any help. Heckler showed her Penny Noble's photograph, then showed it to her associates. One of the three saleswomen who glanced at the picture had been working Wednesday evening, but she only recognized the woman from the *Post*. She did not recall ever seeing Penny shopping at Altman's.

The same thing occurred at Macy's. One person in the lingerie department had been there Wednesday night, but she didn't remember Penny Noble wandering through.

His last shot was Sachet, the lingerie boutique Christine had described in Herald Square. The store was on one of the mall's upper levels, but its location on that level was perfect from a sales standpoint: it was directly across from the up escalator.

The place was empty when Heckler arrived, so he spent a second examining g-strings. When the second became a moment and he realized he was fondling the piece of silk instead of examining it, he tossed the g-string back on the rack and rushed to the sales counter, where he introduced himself to the owner, a slim, attractive woman in her mid forties. Heckler wondered briefly which of her wares she wore under her demure print dress, and then chastised himself for being such a pervert.

"Yes, she was here Wednesday night," the woman told Heckler with just the slightest hint of a British accent. "She was with a friend."

"Do you remember anything unusual about her?"

"She's the one who was killed, isn't she?"

"That's right."

"When I saw the newspaper, I thought to myself I ought to check the credit card receipt of the woman who had been in the store the previous evening. But it became quite busy as soon as I opened up, and I never did get around to it."

"Would you like to check the receipt now?"

"Oh, I don't need to. That's a very good photograph you have. I'm quite sure it's the same woman."

"Could you check anyway? Please."

The woman forced a polite smile, and then excused herself. She returned a moment later with an index-card file box covered with a flowered upholstery.

"Ah, here we are," she said, handing to Heckler the blue American Express card carbon and a sales receipt.

He noted that Penny Noble had spent one hundred and sixty-four dollars on lingerie, including forty-eight dollars for a bustier. He also saw the card was under her maiden name, Graves, indicating it was not a joint account with Gordon.

"Let me go back to my first question," Heckler said. "Do you remember anything unusual?"

The shopkeeper paused thoughtfully. "Well, I'm not exactly sure what you mean by unusual. But I don't think she said anything peculiar."

"Was she happy or sad? Was she irritable? Was she having fun? All those things could be helpful."

"As I recall, she was having fun. They were both having fun. She and her friend."

"What do you mean by fun?"

"They thought what they were doing was really rather naughty. If I hadn't noticed right away that the woman was wearing a wedding band, I would have thought that they were picking out her trousseau. They were really quite nice people."

"Do you remember exactly anything they said?"

"No. Just a lot of, 'Oh, this is perfect,' or 'Won't this slay him.' That sort of thing. They both had a lovely time here."

"And they left together?"

"Yes, I believe so."

Heckler thanked the woman and left his card, urging

her to call him if she remembered any other details, no matter how insignificant they seemed to her.

Mindy Lombardo was the closest thing Harris Cohn had had to a girlfriend. She worked as a secretary in the administration at the New School on Twelfth Street, but she wanted to be a model. Early twenties, bleached blond hair, not quite pretty enough to ever make it as a model, but just pretty enough to keep trying.

Heckler met with her mid afternoon in a New School conference room. For a long time she just talked in a soft, distant monotone about Harris Cohn. She liked him, she didn't love him, but he wasn't a bad sort. They had slept together periodically, but it wasn't a regular thing. He updated her portfolio for her every other month, free of charge, because they were friends. Not because she slept with him once in a while, she insisted.

"Did Harris have any enemies?" Heckler finally asked, realizing he would have to broach the subject sooner or later.

"No, I don't think so," Mindy said quietly.

"Do you know if he sold drugs?"

"No, I don't think Harris was into that."

Heckler sighed. "Mindy, you don't need to protect Harris. The man is dead. The best thing you can do for him now is to help me. Because the more you help me, the better chance I have of finding out who killed him."

"What? Do you think I'm lying?"

"No, I don't, Mindy. But I'm frustrated. We did find traces of cocaine in his apartment, but we don't know if he actually sold. We know he used to take nude portraits, but we can't find his records—prints, or receipts, or a ledger book, perhaps."

"Is that all you're looking for?" Mindy asked, surprised.

"It would be a big help."

"You should have asked. I honestly don't know if he sold drugs. I'm not into that kind of thing personally, and he never offered me any anyway. But his photo business, that's another story. It was all aboveboard, all legal—more or less—but he still had to be very careful. Because nude portraits can really make people mad. Not the model. But, like, the model's ex-boyfriend maybe. Or the model's husband. Or the model's parents—that happened a couple of times. One guy beat the heck out of Harris last year, because Harris took nude photographs of his sister. And the guy found out. He was a truck driver out in Queens."

"Do you know his name?"

"No."

"Would you recognize his picture?"

"No, I never saw him. But Harris told me about it. That sort of thing happened to Harris a couple of times."

"Did I understand correctly before that you said you knew where he kept his old prints and negatives? And his business records?"

Mindy smiled wistfully, and shook her head. "I thought the NYPD never missed a trick."

"What did we miss?" Heckler said quickly. "I'm dying."

"Harris had to protect himself, so he was very careful. But he kept everything, almost like a squirrel. If you go to the wall the couch is on, and go to the side nearest the bedroom, you'll see a seam in the wallpaper. It's where it looks like two pieces meet. But the seam isn't really a seam, it's like a door. Harris built it last fall, after he got beat up and some guy busted his camera. Behind that door will be whatever stuff Harris thought he had to hide. I don't know exactly what's back there, but I guess you'll find whatever receipts or negatives he kept around."

"How big is this space?"

"I don't know, I'm not real good with spaces. But I'd guess it's about a foot deep, and maybe a couple feet high."

"A couple feet?" Heckler asked, incredulous.

Mindy shrugged, looking over Heckler's shoulder at the window behind him. "We all have stuff we'd like to hide. Maybe Harris had more stuff than the rest of us."

15

Breaking Down in a Beige BMW

Gordon's brother answered the door at Gordon's apartment and smiled when he saw Lisa.

"I'm not going to pretend I remember your name," he said easily. "I don't. But I do recall you were the only bridesmaid who could dance."

Lisa smiled back. "It's Curtis, right?"

"Okay, fine, make me feel even guiltier than I already do."

"It's Lisa Stone," she said, extending her hand.

"Well. Come in."

Lisa recalled that Curtis was four years younger than Gordon, but he could almost have passed for a twin. They had the same heavy bones, thinning blond hair, and gray-blue eyes. He was wearing a crew neck sweater and khakis.

"I imagine you know why I'm here," she said.

"I have a pretty good idea. Gordon is getting dressed right now. We're about to drive out to East Hampton to finalize the—," he paused briefly before continuing— "the arrangements."

"How is Gordon feeling?"

"Bad to rotten, I think. He acts collected, but that's just because he has details he can immerse himself in. After tomorrow, when there's no funeral to plan, I think he'll get a lot worse."

"What does he have to do this afternoon? I would have thought by now that most of the details would have been arranged."

Curtis shook his head. "Gordon is going along with the idea of burying Penny in her family's plot in East Hampton, but he isn't happy about it. For one thing, the minister giving the eulogy hadn't seen Penny since she was ten. That's why we're driving out there now. Gordon wants to meet with the minister and go over the eulogy line by line."

"Gordon feels up to that?"

"No, Gordon doesn't," Gordon Noble said, entering the living room where they were standing. "Gordon would much rather have a limb removed than have tea with the portly minister, R. Ronald Nigroni."

Gordon was in the midst of slipping his arm through the sleeve of his blazer. For a moment Lisa was nonplussed, having forgotten how large Gordon was: not fat, or even muscular. Just tall and thick and sturdy.

"Gordon, I'm so sorry for you," Lisa said, going to him finally. She wrapped her arms around him and hugged him, saying, "I'm so sorry."

"I know you are," he said softly, patting her shoulder blade. "I would wager that this has been as difficult for you and Christine as it has been for me."

"How are you holding up, Gordon?"

He shrugged. "I'm doing as well as can be expected. I have neither collapsed sobbing on the couch nor railed unreasonably at the heavens. I'm still here. And that in itself seems to me to be an accomplishment."

"Do you want some coffee, Lisa?" Curtis asked. "Tea?"

"Is there time? I wouldn't want to hold you up."

"Honestly, Lisa, there isn't time," Gordon said. "But I'd much prefer to see you than the head of the First Church of the Holy Brunch. So please, sit."

"Are you sure it's all right?"

"Quite sure."

Curtis took Lisa's and Gordon's requests for coffee, then excused himself. As he left, Lisa sat down on the couch, and Gordon took the chair beside it.

"Curtis thinks my trek out to Long Island today is a bit of energetic nonsense," Gordon confided when Curtis was in the kitchen. "Another way of keeping busy."

"Do you think it will be worth it? Honestly?"

"I wouldn't waste the effort if I didn't think so. I have spoken to Nigroni three times on the telphone, and it's clear to me that the man knows nothing about Penny. My God, if I don't stop him he'll begin with something monstrous, like a Robert Frost poem."

"Why is he doing the eulogy, in that case?"

"Because Penny's parents love the man, and they're insisting that he handle the memorial. I almost think it's their way of making up to him for the fact that Penny and I had someone else officiate at our wedding." Gordon looked up at the ceiling and rolled his eyes. "This could be a very long meeting," he said.

"How are Penny's parents?" Lisa asked.

"Bad. They're not doing well at all. And the tabloids certainly aren't helping them."

"No, I guess they wouldn't."

"Some moments it seems they're more upset about the way their daughter died than by the simpler, more horrendous fact that their daughter is dead. Right now I think they hate the media more than whoever murdered Penny."

"I can't say I blame them. The newspapers haven't been very kind."

Gordon raised an eyebrow. "What a delicate way of phrasing it."

"Okay, they've been cruel. No more euphemisms. They've been rotten."

"Thank you," Gordon said. "Candor is important now."

"You know, Gordon, one of the reasons I'm here is to talk about the press." Lisa took a breath before continuing. "We both know that the media are taking advantage of Penny's death, really sensationalizing it. I think they've given a very distorted picture of your wife. And my friend."

Gordon stared at her, unmoving, arms folded across his chest. Coolly, without passion, he gave her his complete attention. If anyone could murder his own wife, Lisa decided, it was the Gordon Noble of that expression.

"So what I would like to do," she went on, "is to write a story countering the lies in the newspapers. A remembrance, sort of, of the Penny we knew. Something to dispute the image they're presenting of some kind of depraved party girl: 'socialite with a double life' and all."

"Where would you place this article?"

"If possible, *New York* magazine. They're always interested in this kind of thing. But if I struck out there, I could try the *New York Times Sunday Magazine* or the *Village Voice*. There are plenty of places."

"Well, three anyway."

"I think I could get something printed. Something that would vindicate Penny."

"What do you want from me?" Gordon asked evenly.

"Just memories. Whatever you want to recall about your life with Penny," Lisa said cautiously. If anything was going to antagonize Gordon, she knew it would be her next phrase. "Whatever you know about the events that led up to her death."

For a long moment Gordon was silent. Finally he smiled just the tiniest bit and said tiredly, "I can't see any reason not to write it. Would I be able to see whatever you scribble before you submit it?"

"Absolutely."

Curtis returned to the living room with three coffees, setting the tray on the table in front of the couch.

"I'll be happy to talk with you about Penny as much as I can, as long as I can," Gordon said in a tone that sounded almost conspiratorial. "Of course I have no idea how long that will be. I imagine something any minute now will reduce me to some pathetic, quavering wreck. Some memory, some arcane detail.

"But in any event, I'll share with you whatever I can, if you will do me one favor in return."

"Certainly, Gordon. What can I do? Name it."

He looked at his wedding band and began to roll it around his finger. "Come with me to East Hampton this afternoon, and talk to R. Ronald Nigroni. I never knew Penny in college. You did. Your memories of her at Crosby could be a tremendous asset to this man, and do wonders for his eulogy. Perhaps make it palatable."

Lisa smiled to herself. This was an easy request, an opportunity actually, since it would give her four hours in a car with Gordon Noble. The thought did cross her mind that it might be dangerous to spend that much time with Gordon if he really had murdered his wife, but then she looked over at Curtis, and the thought passed. How dangerous could it be if Curtis was with them?

"Is that all?" Lisa asked.

"That's all."

"Well, I would be happy to, Gordon. When do we leave?"

"As soon as we finish our coffee," Curtis told her.

"You know, Lisa," Gordon continued, "you'll also be doing Curtis a great service by coming with me."

"How is that?"

"See those three address books?" Curtis explained to Lisa, pointing at a pile by the breakfront. "There must be twenty to twenty-five people in them I still have to phone and tell how to find the church in East Hampton. If you're going to be keeping Gordon company, I can stay here and wrap up those calls."

Lisa nodded nervously, and said, "So it'll just be me and Gordon."

"You don't mind, do you?" Gordon asked.

"No, of course not," Lisa lied.

"I'm glad. For a moment there, it looked like it would kill you to be with me."

* * *

The sun was beginning to set in the rearview mirror of Gordon's BMW when they finally reached the Long Island Expressway. Lisa recalled reading in an ad somewhere that it took a craftsman over one hundred hours to sew a BMW's leather interior together, and wondered if there wasn't a better way to utilize that much effort. After all, the machine-stitched nylon seats in her family's Catalina were every bit as comfortable as the BMW's, and didn't look half bad for twenty-plus years old. Gordon's BMW was beige, almost the same color as his pants.

"This should open up fairly soon," Gordon said, referring to the traffic on the expressway. "Rush hour is just beginning. If we had gotten here fifteen or twenty minutes later, you would have gotten to see a real disaster. We would have been creeping along at this point at about five miles an hour."

Lisa told herself that any fear she felt was unfounded. Did she really believe that there was even the slightest chance that Gordon Noble, Park Avenue attorney, had murdered his wife? Of course she didn't. Penny was murdered by some enemy of Harris Cohn's, and she was murdered because she was in the wrong place at the wrong time.

And yet there was a queasiness in her stomach that wouldn't settle. And she knew that her voice didn't sound right. It sounded nervous.

"Did you tell Mark where you would be this evening?" Gordon asked casually.

"I didn't speak to Mark. I spoke to his secretary. But I gave her all the details."

"Good. Mark is a real worrier, and I would hate to be responsible for upsetting him."

"Curtis knows where we are. I'm sure he'll tell Christine and Melanie and anyone else who needs to know," Lisa went on, more to reassure herself than explain anything to Gordon.

For the first hour of their drive, neither Lisa nor Gordon brought up Penny. Gordon asked polite questions about advertising, or Lisa asked polite questions about the law, or one or the other would comment again on the traffic. The further they got from Manhattan, however, and the darker the car became, the more willing Gordon became to talk about Penny. By the time they exited the highway at East Hampton, Lisa felt she knew how Gordon and Penny had spent their Sunday afternoons (and who got which sections of the Sunday *Times* first), and which restaurants were their favorites for brunch (and, as a result, which restaurants were most likely to have avocado on any given Sunday). It seemed to Lisa that Gordon appreciated Penny's knowledge of balsamic vinegar and chutney as much as he appreciated any of her talents, and that he was very impressed with her ability to keep conversations moving at dinner parties where no one knew anyone.

But there had not been a whole lot of passion in their marriage, Lisa concluded; Christine was right. Which was strange, because Penny had been a passionate woman. Perhaps it was Gordon's natural tone, but he even sounded a little bored when he talked about Penny, as if he found the memories tiresome.

She was glad she had changed into her commuting Reeboks when she left the office to meet Melanie and Christine. If she had to run, she was wearing sneakers.

They stayed at the rectory almost two hours, not leaving until close to eight-thirty that night. Nigroni's wife, an East Hampton housewife in a madras skirt and espadrilles, had asked them to stay for dinner, but Gordon had refused. Saturday was going to be a long day, he had said, and he wanted to go home and go to bed.

Lisa had offered to drive, but Gordon had insisted that he was better off concentrating on the road than he was staring off into the woods. As they backed out of the rectory driveway, Gordon mumbled that he thought their meeting with the minister had been a success.

"You think so?" Lisa asked, unimpressed with Nigroni and unsure of what they had accomplished.

"I do, yes. I think the man has a much better understanding of Penny now. He knows why she worked at Dayton-Patterson, why she went to Crosby—not just the facts."

Lisa nodded, but as far as she could tell, all Nigroni knew now that he didn't know before were the names of Penny's favorite books and movies. Instead of beginning with Robert Frost, he might now open with Ann Beattie—if he had any Beattie in his library, which wasn't likely.

When they reached the highway and started west, Lisa sat back against the seat and closed her eyes. "Gordon?" she began, trying desperately to keep her voice even, her tone unthreatening, "can I ask you a very personal question?"

"You can. I might not answer it."

"That's fair," she said. She folded her hands across her lap, as if she were trying to get comfortable before dozing off.

"You've told me a lot about Penny—your Penny, I guess—and a lot about your marriage. But we haven't talked about—about what happened."

"Her murder," Gordon said, sighing.

"Yes. Can we talk about that? Are you up to that?"

"Is this for your article? Or for you?"

"Does it matter?" Lisa felt the car accelerating.

"It shouldn't, should it." It was a statement, not a question.

"No. But I guess I'm asking for me. For now, anyway."

"Ask whatever you want then. I'll tell you whatever I want."

She felt the car sway slightly to the left, and considered opening her eyes. But no, they were only changing lanes. "What do you think Penny was doing with Harris Cohn?"

"I know exactly what she was doing with him. She was having some erotic photographs taken."

Lisa was silent. Should she acknowledge that she knew that too, or act surprised, she wondered.

"You didn't know that?" Gordon asked.

"No, I didn't," Lisa lied. "How do you know it?"

"Richard Heckler, a detective, told me. It seems there was a roll of film in Cohn's camera. On it were pictures of Penny in . . . in varying stages of undress."

The BMW bumped when they hit a pothole. "Why did she do that?" Lisa asked.

"Pose for Harris Cohn?"

"Uh-huh."

"I hope it was going to be a birthday present for me."

"The prints, you mean."

"Yes, Lisa. The prints."

"Do you know how she knew Harris Cohn?"

"According to the police, she probably saw one of his ads."

"The man advertised?"

"The man advertised. In the *Village Voice*, I believe they said."

"Do you know who killed her?"

The car began to decelerate, and sway slightly to the right. Lisa opened her eyes and saw they were pulling off to the side of the road. "What are you doing?" she asked. "Do you want me to drive?" Quickly she unfastened her seat belt.

Gordon pushed on the hazard lights when the BMW rolled to a stop.

"What are you doing, Gordon?" she asked again, unable to hide the panic rising in her voice.

He punched on the interior ceiling light and turned to her. He was grinding his teeth.

"Answer me, Gordon, or I'll jump out of this car now, I swear I will."

He reached over and put his hand on her shoulder. "You'll do no such thing," he hissed.

She started to turn to unlatch the door, but Gordon was too fast: with his left arm he grabbed her leg, and through the pressure he applied to her shoulder and her knee he pinned her to the seat.

"You will do no such thing," he went on. "I know what you're thinking, I know what you've thought all night, and I've had it! 'Do I know who killed her?' What the hell kind of question is that?"

It was almost like slow motion, Lisa thought. She could feel her heart racing, but each second seemed to drag on indefinitely. Car after car sped by.

"Don't do anything stupid, Gordon," Lisa finally said after a long, silent moment. "Curtis knows we're together, Mark knows we're together. Nigroni saw us leave together. Every one of those cars out there can see us—"

"What in the name of God do you think I'm going to do?" Gordon yelled at her, cutting her off. "Slash your throat?"

"Let go of me, Gordon," Lisa commanded.

"I'll let go of you when you let go of this paranoid notion that I killed my wife! How dare you think such a thing?"

"Gordon, I never said that."

"No, but you know damn well you thought it. Excuse me, *think* it. It is quite clear that you think I am somehow involved with this whole nightmare as a perpetrator, not a victim. Well, I won't have that anymore. I won't! I have witnesses at the office who know when I left Wednesday night, and I have witnesses at the University Club who saw me playing squash.

"And yet you have the nerve to suggest that I murdered my wife! To be afraid of me! Well, I won't stand for it anymore. I will not stand for it!"

"What do you want from me?" Lisa asked, no less afraid.

"I want," he said, his voice breaking with anger, "I want some understanding. I want some sympathy." His grip loosened, and Lisa realized that he was about to cry. "My wife is dead, don't you understand that? The woman I love is gone. The one soul in the world I wanted to spend my life with. She's gone, Lisa, and she'll never be back!" Slowly he fell against her, resting his forehead on her shoulder. "Oh God," he murmured, "what do I do now?" She wrapped her arms around the big man as best she could, saying nothing, oblivious to the occasional tear that fell on her skirt.

They stopped at a diner midway back to Manhattan for coffee, and ended up ordering cheeseburgers as well. When they were finished, Lisa looked at her watch and saw that it was already close to 11:00 P.M. They would not be back in town until midnight, so Lisa excused herself to phone Mark.

Mark wasn't worried, but he said Melanie was. She had phoned him about ten o'clock and asked that Lisa call her as soon as she could. She was at Lisa's apartment.

Melanie answered the phone on the first ring.

"Mark said you were worried," Lisa began. "Don't be. I'm fine. I'll be back around midnight, I guess."

"Don't go to Mark's, Lisa. Come here, come straight here." Melanie sounded terrified.

"Okay, Mel. I will," Lisa said, trying to soothe her. "What's the matter?"

"This whole thing is beginning to get to me. I'm going a little squirrelly, I think, and I'm really scared."

"What do you mean you're going a little squirrelly?"

"I can't explain it over the telephone."

"Why? No one's tapping my phone, Mel, honest."

"I know that, it's just . . . I'm just scared, that's all. I guess I'm just scared."

"But you are all right?"

"Yes."

"Is Christine all right?"

"Yes."

"You're sure?"

"Of course I'm sure! Just get here as fast as you can! Please!"

"Okay, I'm coming. I'll be there between midnight and twelve-thirty." On a sudden hunch, Lisa then asked, "Is someone with you, Mel? In the apartment?"

"No," Melanie said, almost whining. "That's part of the problem!"

16

The Package
Behind the Wall

The cat had no bones, Heckler was sure of it. The animal draped himself over his lap whenever he sat down to write, his back legs dangling over Heckler's left, his front legs over Heckler's right. The cat was like a shawl.

It was well past midnight when Heckler finally dumped Cubber onto the kitchen floor and scraped some cat food into his dish. Heckler and Cubber had been sitting at Heckler's desk for three hours by then, staring at the facts Heckler had written over and over on the yellow legal pad.

Watching the cat wolf down the canned Purina, Heckler's mind wandered back to Harris Cohn's hiding place. The place was located exactly where Mindy Lombardo had said it was, and it was just about as large. Behind the wall were two metal-ring notebook binders filled with contact sheets and negatives—all of Harris's nude housewives from Greenwich—and a fourteen-ounce package of cocaine with the name Sunshine on it.

The cocaine was pure and uncut, worth anywhere between twenty-five and thirty-five thousand dollars on the open market. Unfortunately, there were no records, no ledgers, no address books. No names, except for Sunshine. Burton had initiated a computer check on the name, but they wouldn't have the results until sometime Saturday morning.

The thing that bothered Heckler, however, was how familiar the name Sunshine was to him as a proper noun. Had he actually known someone somewhere with that name?

Or, perhaps, it was some thing. He had known some thing with the name Sunshine.

Heckler grabbed his windbreaker and keys, and ran out of his apartment, racing down the stairs two at a time. He ran around the corner of his building to the small Korean greengrocer open all night long, and asked where the cleaning products were. The young man pointed behind Heckler, over his shoulder, and there Heckler saw it. Below the Bloom and the Palmolive, beside the Windex and Fab and Fantastik, was Dayton-Patterson's multipurpose window, chrome, and counter cleaner, Sunshine.

17

A Thick Cherry Paste of Flesh and Blood and Muscle

Lisa's apartment was one large room with a small eat-in kitchen, a bathroom, and a walk-in closet on three of the walls, and one wide window facing Gramercy Park on the fourth. Her couch, by far the largest piece of furniture in the room, folded out into her bed. All other pieces of furniture—the china cabinet, the cedar chest, the dining room table—were refurbished art deco items she had acquired over the years. They were lacquered to a slick mahogany finish, providing a startling contrast to the beach-white wicker love seat and easy chair.

When Lisa returned to her apartment a little before 1:00 A.M., she saw that Melanie had made herself at home. The place, usually immaculate, was a mess. There were mounds of cigarette butts in ashtrays, teacups, and coffee mugs, and there were piles of dog-eared magazines scattered around the floor. Melanie's clothes were tossed on every inch of exposed floor and draped from the back of every chair. Melanie herself was sitting cross-legged on the couch thumbing through a month-old *Vogue*. She was wearing Lisa's heaviest fisherman's sweater over her black jeans.

"Good God, Melanie," Lisa said, astounded by the blue haze fogging in her apartment, "I'm amazed the smoke alarm hasn't gone off."

"It did. I took out the battery."

"Melanie, that's just not smart."

"I'm sorry, Lis, but I'm scared. I have to smoke."

"You must have gone through two packs tonight!"

"It was closer to a carton."

Lisa sat down with her on the couch, realizing suddenly just how tired she was. "So why are you upset?" she asked, trying to sound calm and assured.

"Is Mark with you?"

"Do you see him?"

"Of course not. But I thought he might be on his way upstairs now. I thought maybe he was behind you."

"No, I came straight here from the diner. I haven't seen Mark since this morning."

Melanie nodded.

"Is that a problem?" Lisa asked. "Do you want Mark here?"

She shook her head. "No. Just a cigarette."

"So have one. You've already broken the city's anti-pollution laws. One more won't make a difference."

"I don't have any more. I'm all out."

"Melanie, I'm very tired. I can barely keep my eyes open. Why are you scared? Has something happened?"

She looked very young to Lisa, young and vulnerable and childlike. "Not really, nothing specific. Nothing I can explain. But all of a sudden, I'm seeing things, and feeling things. Like tonight I was sure I was being followed. I was sure of it!"

"I've felt that a lot lately also."

"And—and this will sound just plain wacky—but I'm seeing things. I'll look at something, and suddenly it will look like it has blood stains on it. Mark's sweater, Christine's purse, your attaché case. They look like they have these little drops of blood on them!"

"I think we're all a little paranoid right now," Lisa said softly. "I think we just need to get through Penny's funeral tomorrow, and then everything will begin to look up."

"Will you come with me to buy cigarettes?"

"Now? You sound like a junkie."

"I was afraid to go out earlier. Like I said, I thought someone was following me."

"Okay, put your coat on, let's go," Lisa said, rolling her eyes and reaching for her slicker. Her apartment, she decided, smelled like a barroom. And her friend? Her friend smelled like an ashtray. She was just begging for cancer. For chemotherapy, radiation, nuclear medicine, and lasers. For vomiting, baldness, gray skin, and amputation. For death. She became afraid for Melanie, and intuitively sad: Melanie need not fear Penny Noble's killer. She should be so lucky as to die that quickly, with an espresso pot in the skull. No, for better or worse, Melanie had been pegged to take four years to die, throughout her mid thirties, from the time her baby was one until he began nursery school. She would be burned by radiation, scarred by amputation, made hairless by chemotherapy. She would become addicted to morphine, and cry every time she inadvertently rediscovered her hair dyes, gels, and mousses in the back of a closet. Chameleon that she was, she would be reduced perhaps to applying body paint to her naked scalp. That, Lisa decided morosely, was Melanie's fate.

Across the street from Lisa's apartment, Gramercy Park glistened, a dewy mass of trees that sparkled in the moonlight. The place seemed deserted. But as they left Lisa's building and started toward Third Avenue to find an all-night deli, Lisa began to sense they were being watched. Followed. Especially after they left the light from her awning. It was the same sensation she had experienced off and on that afternoon, the feeling that someone was trailing her, stalking her perhaps. She reminded herself that the feeling was unfounded then and was just as unreasonable now. Melanie had frightened her, that was all it was. Yet when she turned around, she was sure that out of the corner of her eye she caught someone lurking in the shadow of her apartment's front door. She wished aloud that her building had a night doorman, but not loud enough for Melanie to hear.

"I wish cities were always this quiet," Melanie said with a sigh, swaying. It was clear she hadn't just been smoking alone, she had also been drinking. If they had to run, Lisa wondered whether Melanie would be able to.

They were halfway down the block when Lisa became convinced that someone was behind them. Instinctively, like an animal, the down on the back of her neck began to bristle. She took Melanie's hand and walked faster, trying to quicken their pace.

"Hey, what's the rush?" Melanie whined.

When Lisa actually heard the footsteps, she turned, but it was too late: the person behind them lunged into Melanie with a rusty carving knife, slamming her into the pavement and slashing her throat from just below her chin to the top of her leather cape. Melanie tried to scream, but when she opened her mouth, Lisa saw it already was filled with a thick red jelly that seemed to choke her. So Lisa screamed for her, and for herself, understanding that the sensation she had felt earlier that evening in Gordon's car was not terror: *this,* she affirmed with each yawning, yodeling yell into the empty park, was terror. Terror was someone in a blue and orange New York Mets ski mask with a foot-long knife, now blood-red. She hit the back of the man's head with her fists and tried once to pull him off Melanie, but her punch was too light to stun him and she was too weak to move him. As she grabbed his shoulders he turned and stabbed her, the knife cutting through her jacket, the shotlike prick against her arm growing into one long gash. It did not hurt as much as Lisa always had imagined a knife wound would hurt, so for the first split second she thought she was all right, that her raincoat had shielded her. But then she saw the knife was coated with more blood, her blood: a thick cherry paste comprised of her flesh and blood and muscle. She thrust her hand inside the tear in her sleeve, running two fingers over the flaps of her wound, and felt an acidic vomit rise in her throat. The man in the ski mask stabbed Melanie twice more in the chest, ripping open her cape to make sure his cuts were thorough, but it was wasted effort: Melanie probably was dead seconds after he had ripped open her neck.

As the killer continued stabbing Melanie, Lisa turned and ran, starting to get dizzy. She was almost to Third Avenue when Ski Mask stood and started after her. Across the avenue and on the other side of Twentieth Street was a Hudson Savings Bank Automatic Teller Machine: indoors, well lit, and open twenty-four hours a day to Hudson Savings convenience customers. Seeing no one on the street to help her, and all traffic in sight stalled at a red light four blocks away, she staggered across the street to the ATM, emptying her purse in the middle of the intersection as she rummaged through it for her wallet and her convenience banking credit card.

American Express and MasterCard, Saks, Bonwit's, and Bloomingdale's were dumped unceremoniously onto the pavement as she ran. Even when she found the gold Hudson Savings card she was searching for, she knew she was not home free. At least half the time the doors malfunctioned and the magic convenience cards were unable to trigger the magnetic locks that opened them. Red "In Process" signs flashed for thirty seconds when the cards were inserted, sometimes longer, and still the doors remained shut tight. Or worse, the opposite might occur: the door would open without inserting a Hudson Savings card. Either way, if the door were broken, Lisa feared she was a dead woman.

And even if it wasn't broken—the door worked perfectly—she might still be in trouble, because for all she knew, Ski Mask banked at Hudson as well. It was a possibility: even psycho killers had to bank somewhere.

She reached the ATM and slipped her card into the slot, cursing. She reached for the door, ready to open it, as Ski Mask galloped across the street thirty yards down the block. She heard a click as the electronic lock shut off, followed by the buzzing that indicated the door could be opened. Her prayers answered, she pulled her card from the slot and rushed into the ATM center, pushing the door shut behind her. She positioned herself smack in the middle of the bright cubicle, directly before the twenty-four-hour camera, and pointed at the video monitor behind her for the benefit of Melanie's killer. She was astounded by her image on the screen: a crying, shaking, disheveled woman with the haircut of a six-year-old boy, standing in a yellow slicker with one arm raised moronically like the Statue of Liberty, the other a limp red and yellow tentacle. The absurdity of her gamble suddenly struck her: she was hoping a maniac would be deterred from bashing through the glass and killing her because he might be on film. And "might" was an especially key word, because she was fairly sure that less than half the ATM cameras actually videotaped the money machines. The rest were decoys. And if Ski Mask was not deterred by the monitor—the likely scenario, Lisa realized—then she had cornered herself.

The killer reached the door and stopped. He looked at Lisa, then at the camera. And then applauded. Putting his knife inside his coat, he actually clapped, nodding his head in approval. Lisa thought he was laughing and tried to see his eyes, but the man averted his gaze before she could focus. He pulled the knife back out of his jacket, pointing the razored tip at Lisa, and then ran back down Twentieth Street toward Gramercy Park.

Lisa stood still for a moment, trying to catch her breath. She knew she was peeing on the floor, could feel the stinging wetness dribble down her legs, could see the pale yellow puddle forming on the tile. She then bent over and threw up, wondering—but not caring—what the Hudson Savings Bank did to customers who pissed and puked in their ATM outlets and left blood stains on the door. Impound their money? Deny them credit? Withdraw their ATM privileges? When she could stand upright again, she staggered to the customer service phone, only to discover that the receiver was not attached to the phone cord. Her strength ebbing, afraid she would bleed to death if she didn't get help, she realized she would have to leave the cubicle alone. She waited until Third Avenue was a mile of green lights and traffic was streaming uptown, and then scampered into the middle of the wide street. Looking around, she saw that Ski Mask really had seemed to have disappeared, and waved at an oncoming taxi. It skidded to a halt within feet of her, and she collapsed onto its hood.

She heard the driver leave his cab and scream at her in Spanish, then gasp when he saw the blood smeared across her coat. Her last conscious thought before darkness enveloped her was that although she was wrong about how Melanie would die—it was quicker than she had anticipated—it was nevertheless a cigarette-related death.

IV

Saturday

18

In the Geriatric Wing

Lisa woke up Saturday morning in the geriatric wing of Bellevue Hospital, her left arm stitched, bound, and taped, her right arm attached intravenously to a Glad Bag of glucose and Valium. On her left was a window and a small night table, and on her right was a plump old woman who, an orderly had told her, had just had brand new pins put in her century-old hips. She was still sleeping.

Judging by the sky, which looked again that day like it might rain or snow, it couldn't have been later than six-thirty. Although the cab driver had taken her to Bellevue within minutes of finding her the night before, by the time the orderlies had taken her upstairs, it was close to 3:00 A.M. She had spent almost two hours in the emergency room.

By daylight, everything that happened the night before was fuzzy. Everything except Melanie's wide, pleading eyes when she was murdered. Those remained vivid, causing Lisa's own eyes to tear. Why, she wondered with a sadness she had never felt before, would someone kill Melanie? Why? She hadn't realized it before, but she knew it now with a certainty that made her whole body shiver: she cared for Melanie as much as she had ever cared for anyone. Oblivious to the woman next to her, she began to cry.

"Oh God, Melanie," she heard herself saying over her soft sobs, "I miss you already."

She tried to recall the details of Melanie's murder and remembered vaguely the ATM cubicle. But she had no conception of how long she had stayed there, or why she had left. All she knew for sure was that a cabby eventually picked her up. She remembered Manny Ortega, the pudgy Puerto Rican driver, trying to pull her out of his back seat. For one very brief second she had panicked, become afraid again, and begun to kick; only when she saw that she was at a hospital had she regained her composure. She had not stopped crying, but neither had she remained hysterical or incoherent. One of the doctors on duty in the emergency room had looked at her wound immediately, but when he saw that it wasn't life-threatening, had given her a sedative and told a huge old nurse shaped like a pear to apply compresses. "Cuts are a bitch," the nurse had said, shaking her head as she tried to console Lisa, "but at least you're not in a diabetic coma. Had one of those earlier tonight. Now *that* was a real bitch."

Although Lisa remembered the parade of people who had visited her in the hospital, she had only vague notions of what she had said to any of them. Within seconds of arriving, even before she could phone Christine, or Mark, or her parents, two police officers already in the emergency room had descended upon her. They had just dropped off a vomiting junkie and were about to leave when Lisa and Ortega staggered in. While the nurse had pressed rough towels against her arm, the police had radioed another car to verify the existence of Melanie's body on Twentieth Street and then begun to fill out a preliminary report. As soon as they were through, a woman in a red and white striped smock had badgered her for her Social Security, Blue Cross, and telephone numbers. Only then had Lisa been allowed to use the phone.

She did not remember whether she had called Christine or Mark first, but she thought it was probably Christine because she had wanted to warn her not to leave

Gordon's apartment alone. Regardless, they had arrived together, a little before two, when the doctor was putting in the first of her forty stitches. Her parents arrived half an hour later, well after the doctor had determined there was little apparent muscle damage. She was nevertheless told to remain overnight for observation, because her body was still in shock. Her mother had hugged her, and her father had railed at an orderly for making her wait so long to be stitched. She would have been given her bed in the geriatric wing—the only available bed in the hospital—at that moment if Richard Heckler had not then arrived. He had rushed to Bellevue as soon as he heard the names of the two victims, recognizing them immediately as Penny Noble's college roommates. When he saw that Lisa would recover, however, he had asked her only a few perfunctory questions, deciding most could wait until the morning.

She vaguely recalled Mark shoving a newspaper reporter in the emergency room at one point, maybe two reporters, but she didn't believe she herself had spoken to them. At any rate, it was 3:00 A.M. by the time she was tucked in bed.

The old woman beside her snored—long, lanquid, gutteral groans. They reassured Lisa, confirmed for her that she was not alone. Granted, the woman could provide absolutely no help if the man in the mask were suddenly to stampede down the tile corridor and crash into her room. But she was at least a presence. Someone to die with her, the way Harris Cohn had died with Penny. There was a real irony there that almost made Lisa smile: all along she had assumed, more or less, that it was Penny who had died because she had gotten involved with Harris Cohn. In all likelihood, however, it was probably the other way around: Cohn was the unknowing, almost innocent victim. There was no doubt in Lisa's mind now that the same person who had killed Penny had killed Melanie. And would try to kill her and Christine. Heckler had said the night before that it was possible, but he would not be sure until he understood the motive. And that was still up in the air.

As the sun rose, it again occurred to Lisa that Gordon Noble had murdered his wife—that Gordon Noble was Ski Mask. But she could not think of any reason why he would want her dead. Her article? Her investigation? It was possible, certainly, but it was not as if she were on the verge of some incriminating breakthrough. At least she didn't think she was. Besides, she reminded herself, that wasn't why she was writing the article in the first place. She wasn't "after" anyone. All she wanted to do was cleanse Penny's legacy. At least that was all it was at the beginning. She wasn't so sure anymore.

Now all she knew for sure was that someone had tried to kill her and that the knowledge angered her as much as it frightened her. It was, she thought, a sensation similar to being told you have some sort of inoperable condition: the sword of Damocles had become for her the steak knife of Ski Mask. It was an infuriating sensation, the idea that for no apparent reason there was every chance she would die. It was unjust, unsportsmanlike, unfair. It was insufferable. It was a cheat. She did not, after all, deserve to die. She had done nothing wrong, harmed no one; she had kept her lying, cheating, and stealing to a minimum, and honored her mother and father as much as humanly possible, given who they were.

She tried to recall the series of emotions through which terminal patients passed, believing that she had read somewhere that rage typically followed denial but preceded haggling and final acceptance. Unwilling to progress to haggling (and admittedly unsure of whether she had properly experienced denial), she pressed the small button on the bed by her right hand, summoning the nurse. She was enraged all right, but she decided she would channel that hostility into a plan for survival.

A nurse arrived in a few minutes, an Asian woman about Lisa's age.

"Good morning," she whispered from the foot of the

bed. Her name was Tami, according to the pin on her dress.

"Hello," Lisa said, astounded by the feeble airiness of her voice. She could barely speak. "Time?"

"Seven-fifteen. How do you feel?"

"Tired."

"Are you hungry? I think you could have a light breakfast."

"No. Don't want breakfast."

"Do you hurt?" She circled around to the window side of the bed and glanced at Lisa's arm. "You don't seem to need a new dressing. There's only a minimum of fluid."

"I want," Lisa said, carefully articulating each word, "company. I want to use the telephone."

"That's easy." She bent Lisa's right arm for her, showing her that despite the IV she could move it, and placed the receiver in her right hand. "What number can I dial?"

Lisa gave her Mark's number. He answered after three rings, sounding himself like death. Raspy, sickly, and exhausted.

"Can you come here?" she asked him.

"I was planning on coming right there," he said, his voice becoming softer with concern. "How are you? How do you feel?"

"I'm tired. My arm hurts. Mostly I'm mad. Scared, but mad."

"Are they going to let you out today?"

Lisa looked at Tami and inquired, "Am I going home today?"

"Maybe."

"Maybe," Lisa said.

"We need to talk about that," Mark told her.

"I know. I can't be alone."

"Probably not. But we'll figure that out. God, I've been worried about you."

"I'm fine."

"You sound a little spacey."

"A lot spacey. I'm a lot spacey. Everything's blurry still."

"That's probably good."

"You sound pretty spacey yourself."

"Just tired. I sat up with your parents until about five this morning."

"Where was Christine?" she asked suddenly, wondering why he hadn't said Christine was with them. "Is Christine all right?"

"She stayed at the hotel last night with your parents. She's fine."

"Thank God," she said, relieved. She noticed that Tami wanted her off the phone so she could go about her business. "Mark," she said again, "please hurry. Please."

"I will," he told her, and then added, "I love you."

The words surprised her. He had never told her that before, and she had never had an inclination to say it to him. Reflexively she almost told him that she loved him too, but she could not bring herself to say it. Instead she said stupidly, "Thank you," and handed the phone receiver to Tami. She wished immediately after she had said the words that she could take them back, because they must have sounded so cruel to Mark. And for all she knew, maybe she did love Mark, or could or would love him someday. She almost wanted to call him again to take the "thank you" back and tell him anything else. Tell him she didn't mean to be cruel, but that she was too busy being scared to death to worry about other people's feelings. Tell him, perhaps, that she did love him. Or could or would love him someday.

"Can I have some company?" Lisa asked Tami. "I don't want to be alone."

"Visiting hours begin at ten o'clock. But we have candy stripers here as early as eight who could sit with you. Can you wait until then?"

"No."

"I see. Let me go to the desk and see if there's someone sitting around with forty minutes to spare. Okay?"

"Okay."

But before Tami returned with company, Lisa fell back to sleep.

19

"Crosby-Slaughter"

Lisa opened her eyes and stared up at Richard Heckler's hair. She had thought that only eight-year-olds and mass murderers had crew cuts.

"Morning," Heckler said, grinning. "Feeling better?"

"Better than what?"

Heckler shrugged. "Just better, I guess."

"No. I feel lousy." She wondered if he was leering, and looked away. Scanning the room she saw Tami, the nurse, changing the sheets on the next bed. "Where is the old woman?" Lisa asked, seeing the bed was empty.

"On the fourth floor, in therapy," Tami answered. "She's learning to walk with a walker."

"Where is everyone else?" She didn't think it was quite fair that she had woken up to a police detective instead of Mark or her family.

"Kith and kin are all downstairs in the coffee shop, savoring Bellevue's renowned cinnamon toast," he explained, rubbing the bed's metal guardrail with his thumb.

"Oh."

"Don't be disappointed. They'll be here as soon as we've had a chance to talk."

"That's fine."

Heckler looked at Tami and with a slight nod of his head asked her to leave. He then turned back to Lisa, saying, "I want you to know, I'm sorry about waking you up. Sleep is probably the best thing in the world for you right now."

"What time is it?"

"Not quite nine o'clock," Heckler said, pausing. "You really don't feel very good?"

"No, I really don't feel very good."

Heckler pulled a toothpick from his blazer pocket and rolled it between his fingers. "Well, do you feel up to a chat?" he asked with a singsong bop in his voice.

"Sure," she said tiredly. "Go ahead, ask whatever you want."

Heckler questioned Lisa for close to thirty minutes. He asked her about the Penny she knew at Crosby and the Penny who married Gordon Noble. He wanted to know everything she could recall about the person who killed Melanie and who may have killed Penny. Even standing still, some part of Heckler's body seemed to Lisa to be moving. His fingers tapped his thighs, the mattress, the railing, while his feet tapped the tile floor. He continually switched his toothpick from one side of his mouth to the other.

Finally, a little after nine-thirty, he hopped on to the radiator by the window and sat down. "So tell me," he asked, "what do you know about Sunshine?"

"Is this for botany or biology?"

"It's for cleaning windows."

Lisa rolled her eyes, annoyed. "You want to know what I know about Sunshine window cleaner?"

"That's right."

"I know it's blue."

"That's all?"

"That's all."

"You've never done advertising for it?"

"If you mean, have I ever worked on the brand, then no, I haven't."

"That's what I meant. So you don't know Frank Arnold?"

"No."

"Carol Stuart?"

"No."

"Walt Swaggert?"

Lisa started to repeat the word no, but the name quickly registered. "I've spoken to him on the phone. He used to work on Sunshine."

"That's right. Up until early last year. He was followed by Carol Stuart, who was followed by Frank Arnold. I believe they're called 'brand managers.'"

Lisa nodded. "What does Walt Swaggert have to do with this?"

"Probably nothing. They all probably have nothing to do with this. But we found about thirty thousand dollars worth of uncut coke in a brown package in Harris Cohn's apartment. In an honest-to-God secret compartment. And the only name on the package was the word Sunshine."

Lisa looked out the window. "I imagine you know Penny used to work on Sunshine," she said.

"Yup, sure do."

"And you think that cocaine was for Penny."

"Maybe. I can tell you think so."

"Not necessarily. Penny didn't take drugs."

"But the thought crossed your mind."

"Briefly. But it didn't make sense."

"That's what Christine said too. Your friend. You both tell me that Penny Noble didn't take drugs, you say she wasn't into that kind of thing. But the fact is, she was found dead in a drug dealer's apartment, her body not twelve feet from a package with her name on it."

"You told me the package said Sunshine. Not Noble."

"You're right," Heckler said softly. "That was an unfair leap. A circumstantial leap. So tell me this. What does a brand manager do?"

Lisa sighed. "Runs the business. As the title says, manages the brand."

"Pretend you're talking to a ten-year-old, Lisa. I have no idea what that means."

"There are a lot of things involved with selling a shampoo, or paper towels. Or a window cleaner," she said, trying to clear her head. "You have packaging to worry about: does the cap fit properly on the spray nozzle? There are promotions: is a twenty-five-cent coupon enough to make Grand Union and A & P happy? Someone has to make sure the sales force has what it needs, and the ad agency isn't sitting on its hands. Someone has to formulate the marketing plans and sell them to management. Figure out sales goals and then reach them. That's the sort of thing brand managers do. Basically, they take responsibility for all the day-to-day management of one particular brand."

"Doesn't sound like the sort of job where you would need a whole lot of cocaine, does it?"

"No, it doesn't. It isn't."

"So it isn't likely she was buying cocaine for some job-related activity."

"No. Especially at Dayton-Patterson," Lisa answered, wondering suddenly if there were more behind Melissa Hayes's unwillingness to speak with her than simple corporate reticence. "They're a very conservative company," she added with some hesitation, hoping that Heckler didn't detect the doubt in her voice.

Heckler hopped off the radiator. "Look, Lisa, we don't know for sure that Penny went to Harris Cohn's on Wednesday to buy cocaine," he said gently, looking into Lisa's eyes. "But we do know for sure that one of the reasons she was there was to have him take her picture, nude. Was that in character with the Penny Noble you knew?"

"No, not really."

"I didn't think so. And yet you don't seem surprised."

"I'm not. But I was when I first found out."

"When was that?"

Lisa paused, concentrating. "Gordon told me about them—the pictures," she answered. It wasn't a lie, she reasoned, since Gordon really had told her about them. It was just that Christine had told her about them first.

Heckler nodded before continuing. "What I'm getting at, Lisa, is that there may have been a side to Penny Noble that neither you nor Christine nor Gordon ever saw. And learning about that side could be a big help in putting this whole affair to bed."

"I've told you everything I can remember about Penny—"

"Oh, I believe that," Heckler said, cutting her off. "And I believe Christine and Gordon have told me everything they can remember. It's just that the pieces don't fit."

"What do you think happened?" Lisa asked, staring up at the ceiling.

"I don't have one theory, I must have fifteen. Unfortunately, I have no suspects. Not one of my little theories answers the question, who killed Penny Noble and Harris Cohn. Or Melanie Braverman."

"Can you tell me them anyway?"

"My theories?"

"That's all. What you think."

"Well, let's see. There's the Cohn route: someone wanted to ice Cohn, and your friend picked a bad time to pose . . . or score some toot. Whatever. Your other friend, Melanie, then, was a whole other issue. Coincidence. Victim of a serial killer, maybe.

"But then again, maybe she wasn't a coincidence. Maybe she knew something.

"Then there's the Noble route: someone wanted to waste your friend, and Cohn happened to be the unlucky attendee. Again, Melanie Braverman is a related homicide only because she stuck her nose in something nasty.

"And then there's the Crosby route: the same dude who murdered Penny murdered Melanie, and he did so just because they were friends, or because they lived together once, or because they went to Crosby. But they had something in common. This route again means that Cohn was just one unlucky guy. It also means," he added matter-of-factly, "that you, Christine, and God knows who else are in danger."

Lisa stretched her legs, annoyed at Heckler's casual acknowledgment that she was in jeopardy. A little more concern seemed to be in order. "You know that whoever killed Penny, killed Melanie. I don't think it would take Machiavelli to figure that out."

"Machiavelli might jump to that conclusion, but Columbo wouldn't. Nor would Baretta, Friday, Belker, McMillan and Wife, Cagney and Lacey, Simon and Simon, or Andy of Mayberry. No way.

"And even if that conclusion is right—and let's face it, Lisa, it probably is—what does that tell us? Does it tell us that Gordon Noble hired someone to murder his wife while he played squash at the University Club? No. Does it tell us that some irate crack addict wasted Harris and Penny? No again. Does it tell us that some psycho is roaming the streets knifing former Crosby students for no apparent reason? No, no, and no," Heckler said, breaking abruptly into a smile. "Of course, the *New York Post* would disagree with me. They believe it's a simple case of an anti-Crosby psychopath."

"I haven't seen today's paper," Lisa said nervously. "What does it say?"

"You, Lisa Stone, are a media celebrity."

"Oh God, no. I'm not in the *Post*, am I?"

"Sure are. And the *Times*."

"How awful is it? Do you have a *Post* here? I have to see one!"

"It's not that bad at all, it's harmless. There's one right outside in the waiting room."

"Could you get it? Please?"

"In time. I just want to go over one more thing."

"Fine, fine, fine then," Lisa mumbled into her pillow, astounded by the way her life was unraveling. In three days, two friends had been murdered, someone had tried to kill her, and she was probably being raped that very moment in today's papers.

"Penny's funeral is this afternoon," Heckler said, "I have no objection to your going to it. But as soon as it's through, I think you should leave town."

"Leave town?"

"Absolutely."

Leave town. The idea infuriated Lisa. She had assumed the police would provide her with protection. "I thought somebody would look out for me! You said yourself I'm in danger!"

"I know I did," Heckler said, nodding and spreading out his arms. "But how much protection do you think we can give you? Should we send a uniform to be your bodyguard? And one for your friend from Atlanta? And one for every other Crosby graduate who will be in East Hampton this afternoon?"

"It's different for Christine and me," Lisa said. "You know that. We're the ones who lived with Penny and Melanie. Just us. You know you wouldn't have to find bodyguards for half of Crosby College!"

"No argument. I just want you to see the whole picture," he said, kicking his heel against the radiator. "We can't give you full-time protection. We just can't do it. Sure, we would have extra blues cruising Gramercy Park, we could give you rings on the hour, even drop by your building a couple times a day. Make sure you're all right. But that's not a perfect shield. That's not a safety net, it's a fishnet. A tuna net. That's how big the holes are. If someone wants you dead, he could walk through them upright they're so big."

"But if I left town, I'd have no protection."

"Depends on where you go. Isn't there some place where you could drop out of sight for four or five days? That's all, just four or five days. So we can get a handle on this."

Her first thought was Bronxville, but the village was

only twenty-five minutes from Manhattan by train. Besides, she did not want to involve her family.

"What about my arm?" she asked. "Don't I have to be near doctors?"

"If you're wimpy."

"What the hell does that mean?"

"It means no. I spoke to the doctors this morning. They said if you're coherent, and functioning, and not too screwed up by what you witnessed last night, you could hit the road."

"My arm really hurts!"

"So would an espresso pot in the head. Or a cut across your throat. Your stitches are sound. You can travel."

"Is that a medical opinion, or your opinion?"

"Look," he said calmly, "you seem pretty damn together, given what you've been through. So use your head. A doctor will check out your arm again in a few minutes. If he says it's cool to leave, my recommendation—my humble recommendation—is to split. Go to Penny's funeral, there will be a lot of people there. But then scram. Hightail it out of the Apple. That's just a recommendation, take it or leave it. If you can, you should go."

There was always New Hampshire. She could run to the Stones's summer home in Sugar Hill. It would provide a six-hour buffer zone between herself and New York City.

"My family has a home in New Hampshire. In the White Mountains."

Heckler snapped his fingers. "Perfecto."

Perfecto. This man, Lisa thought, would have been perfecto for Melanie. "I assume you want me to leave tonight?"

"I want you and someone else to leave tonight. No sense in your being alone up there."

"I agree. I would be afraid to be alone."

"Understandable."

"What if I left tomorrow?"

"I wouldn't wait that long. I'd leave as soon as possible, if I were you."

"What about Christine?"

"She's going to return to Atlanta, with any luck this evening. I've already spoken to her. If you two really are likely targets—as you think—it's best to separate you. And I can't think of a better way to do it than to send one southbound and one northbound."

"That's all there is to it? I call the office and say I'm not coming in this week, get in the car, and drive to New Hampshire?"

"That's it."

That's it. She could just imagine herself phoning Jack O'Donnell, the account director, and explaining she wouldn't be in that week because a maniac was trying to kill her, perhaps because she went to a women's college, or perhaps for no reason at all. It was all in the *Post*.

"Could I see the newspapers now?" she asked. "I might as well know what the world will think I'm running from."

"I trust that means you're leaving?"

"Probably. But no promises."

"Is that the best you'll do?"

"For now."

"Okay," he said, heading for the door, "it's your life. Let me get you that *Post*, and then I'll commandeer your parents."

Heckler returned a moment later, shaking his head at the *Post*'s headline, and mumbled again that he would go downstairs to find her family. As soon as he left, Lisa sat up slightly in bed, using only her right elbow for leverage, and began to read. Although she was expecting the face on the front page this time, Lisa nevertheless felt the same dizziness she had experienced when she was surprised by Penny Noble's picture two days earlier. The photograph, in all likelihood taken from Melanie's wallet, was recent. She had no idea what color Melanie's hair was in the picture, since it was black and white, but she did know that the bug-eyed checkerboard sunglasses that served as her hair clip were relatively new. Lisa remembered that Melanie had bought them in a nostalgia boutique in Soho only six months ago, when she had been in town for Penny's wedding.

The four-word headline, all large block letters, elicited from Lisa one small squeak of astonishment: "Yuppie Slain on Sidewalk." The callousness of the generalization appalled her, and she stared at the word for half a minute. More than anything else, even more than the way the word "sidewalk" was capable of frightening her now because she associated it with a knife-wielding maniac in a blue and orange ski mask, the paper's use of the word "yuppie" hurt her feelings.

There was no teaser paragraph on the front page that day, but there was a smaller subhead: "Crosby-Slaughter Continues." Unlike Penny, Melanie did not have the entire front page to herself. In a red column down the left side of the page was a promotion for the *Post*'s new Wingo "Be a Billionaire" game. Something about being an instant winner on "The Bettor Bus to Atlantic City." Turning to the inside pages, she saw that the paper only had time to fill one page with "Crosby-Slaughter" stories.

There were two articles, a longer one about the murder and a shorter sidebar about Crosby College. The first one, "Second Crosby Grad Savagely Murdered in Gramercy Park," had a photograph of the southern gates of Gramercy Park at night. Evidently, Melanie's body had been removed by the time the photographers had arrived. The smaller story, "Crosby College: Ivy League Girl's School," had a stock photograph of Jeremy Browning Hall, the college's large gothic auditorium. Each article had the small "Crosby-Slaughter" logo, a rendition of a Doric-columned administration building that could belong to any northeastern Ivy League school, with a bolt of jagged lightning through it.

She read the longer article first:

Melanie Braverman, 27, has become the latest victim in the grisly murders detectives now refer to as "Crosby-Slaughter." She was found brutally murdered on East 20th Street late last night, stabbed multiple times in the face, neck, and chest.

Like Penelope Noble, executed with infamous pornographer Harris Cohn last Wednesday, Miss Braverman went to Crosby College and in fact roomed with Mrs. Noble there for a few years.

Miss Braverman was a graphic designer who lived in Boston, Massachusetts. She was not married.

Another Crosby woman who was with Miss Braverman when she was stabbed to death, Lisa Stone, 27, escaped with minor injuries to her arm.

Miss Stone told the police the killer shielded his face with a ski mask with a New York Mets insignia on it.

The crazed madman ambushed Miss Braverman and Miss Stone when they left Miss Stone's apartment on Gramercy Park South for cigarettes just after 1:00 A.M. He jumped the unfortunate pair from behind, and began stabbing Miss Braverman again and again.

Miss Stone tried to stop the masked cutthroat, but he stabbed her down her left arm.

Police believe he would have killed Lisa Stone next, if passing cab driver Emmanuel Ortega hadn't heard Miss Stone's cries for help and come to her aid. But by the time he arrived, their assailant had fled, leaving one woman dead and the other injured.

Ortega immediately took Miss Stone to Bellevue Hospital.

"She was scared to death and bleeding

like crazy, so I just floored it to the hospital," Ortega said.

Miss Braverman, a gorgeous beauty with a model's features, was almost unrecognizable when police recovered her body, because her face had been so gruesomely disfigured.

Police are almost positive that the ghastly murders of Penelope Noble and Melanie Braverman are related, but do not yet have a reason why a homicidal maniac is killing Crosby graduates in cold blood.

"There are several links between the two murders," Detective Richard Heckler said. He would not elaborate any more on the grim similarities.

Police also would not say whether they had any leads at this point, and if so, what they were.

Miss Braverman was described by her friends as a "nice, sweet person," and "a lot of fun to be with." A fellow graphic artist called her "creative."

Miss Stone is an account executive with Ormand, Mathews, and Reiner, one of the world's largest advertising agencies.

It was an odd sensation for Lisa to see her name in the *Post*, rather like reading one's own obituary, she decided. Still, the article would have been much worse if Heckler had not been so tight-lipped. She would have to thank him.

The shorter article, the one about Crosby College, was even more innocuous:

Crosby College is an Ivy League quality women's school just north of Pittsfield, Massachusetts. Its 2,600 students look up to such prestigious alumnae as feminists Rickey Chassmen and Mary Claire-Hunter.

One of the oldest all-women's colleges in the country, Crosby opened in 1888. It gets its name from Thistle Crosby, the wife of a Massachusetts whaler and missionary who left an incredible fortune in her will to endow the school.

The rustic campus is located at the foot of the Berkshire Mountains, and is one of the nation's most beautiful schools. It is also one of the most expensive, with tuition a whopping $16,000 a year!

The college is deep in tradition. The students live in large "houses" instead of dormitories, and often with the same girls for four years.

Every Thursday is "Firelight Supper," when the students invite their boyfriends from other colleges over for romantic, candlelight dinners of roast beef, Yorkshire pudding, and other gourmet foods in their "houses."

But despite these traditions, the college is modern in the way it helps women learn to achieve in business, politics, and the arts and sciences. Many of its graduates now go on to successful careers in banking, insurance, and publishing.

Unfortunately, graduates from the peaceful college are now being stalked by a bloodthirsty madman with some strange vendetta against the college. Dale Masters, dean of students, said they are even worried about their current students.

"We're all in a state of shock. While we don't believe our students are in serious jeopardy right now, we are planning on taking certain security precautions," Masters said.

The article was only eight paragraphs long, she thought, but they still managed to get in a dig about firelight suppers. She put aside the paper, almost smiling, when she heard her parents, Mark, and Christine down the hall.

20

"Preserve Me from the Violent Man"

Early Saturday afternoon, Mark drove Lisa and Christine out to East Hampton, the Long Island town where Penny's funeral was to be held. He had borrowed the car, a cream-colored station wagon with baby toys in the back, from a doctor in his building. Christine sat in the back seat while Lisa sat in the front beside Mark. Occasionally Christine commented on the view from the Triboro Bridge or the Long Island Expressway, or wondered aloud which other women from Crosby would be at the funeral, but most of the time everyone was quiet. It was partly a nervous quiet, because now Melanie was dead too, but it was also the dreary, joyless quiet brought on by all funerals. The ritual seemed to Lisa to be forcing them to accept the absolute finality of Penny's and Melanie's deaths. Separating the way things had been a week earlier and the way they were now was an abyss that could not be bridged. Just as the rock salt that had splashed on Lisa's stockings that morning would never be removed, but had left a mark on the material far more durable than the material itself, so would the plain fact that her college roommates were gone always dominate a small part of her mind.

Sleet had been falling throughout the morning, with the result that all of New York's roads looked like over-turned Slurpees. It was too warm to snow and too cold to rain, as if, Lisa thought, her mood had somehow dictated the weather.

When they reached the church, Mark let the two women out by the front doors and drove past a long line of black Oldsmobiles to the parking lot. There was no canopy or archway, so they immediately ran into the vestibule to escape the sleet. Down the aisle at the front of the church were Penny's parents, her sister, and Gordon. Mrs. Graves was sitting down, facing the casket, while her husband and Gordon stood on either side, whispering. Mr. Graves stood erect, with what appeared to be a steady, even gaze. But Lisa also noticed that his left hand was entrenched in his pants pocket, rattling change. Occasionally, he reached up to twirl what remained of his hair, with the same effort sixty-year-old men used to start fifteen-year-old lawn mowers. Gordon too was striving to project a stoic serenity, and failing in equal measure: while his hands were clasped firmly behind his back, he was swaying like a dying pen-dulum, with jerking, uncoordinated spasms. At one point Penny's mother turned slightly, allowing Lisa to glimpse through the woman's black veil a face with too much rouge and drugged, oblivious eyes.

Spread out behind the front pews, fanning out like a fir tree, were somewhere between seventy-five and one hundred people in black and blue and an occasional brown. An unsubtle babble traveled among them, and a head periodically gestured toward the coffin. The organ was only about fifteen feet from the casket, and although it was separated from it by a wall of flowers, Lisa won-dered whether the organist would think about his prox-imity to the dead woman as he played.

"It's a closed casket," Christine said. "We should have expected that."

Christine was wedged into her black dress like a fat flamenco dancer. "Most of us hadn't given any thought to whether the casket would be open or closed," Lisa answered, but secretly believed the organist had.

"Just an observation, Lis, that's all."

Some faces from the rear pews turned to see who was arriving, and Lisa recognized at least a dozen people. She saw Warren Racine and Jack O'Donnell sitting among what had to be the Dayton-Patterson contingent—a group of men and women wearing an almost identical shade of banker's gray—and she noticed at least two groups of women from Crosby. Some, like Kate Hemmick, she still saw occasionally. Others, like Stacey Penrose, she had not seen in years. She nodded slightly, almost imperceptibly, greeting them all.

"I feel a little conspicuous here," Christine said. "Let's sit down."

"I told Mark we would wait in the back of the church," Lisa told her. She was relatively sure Christine felt uncomfortable because her dress made her look like a human pork sausage. Overweight people—and Christine was no exception—rarely liked drawing attention to themselves.

"Mark seems like a competent adult. He'll find us."

"Fine," Lisa responded, not wanting to fight. "We'll go sit down." She followed Christine to a pew midway toward the front of the church, and the two of them edged past an emotionless couple in their fifties. Probably neighbors of the Graveses with no particular fondness for Penny, Lisa thought. She wondered why Christine chose not to sit with Kate Hemmick, but then realized Christine was probably afraid that if the three of them sat together, they might all wind up hysterical.

When they were seated, Christine clawed Lisa's sleeve and asked urgently, "Did you see him?"

"Did I see who? Gordon?"

"No, not Gordon! Leslie Nichols!" Christine whispered intensely.

"He's here? He came all the way out here for the funeral? From Massachusetts?" She craned her neck to try and find him.

Staring straight ahead Christine said, "Sure did. He's a few rows behind us. But don't turn around, Lis. Take my word for it, he hasn't changed a twit."

An uncomfortable awareness of her physical self spread through Lisa, the sense she had had often that week of being watched. But it was also a vain self-awareness, because suddenly she wished she had chosen to wear navy blue instead of gray. She knew she looked better in blue.

"Just hasn't changed a twit," Christine said again, shaking her head.

Lisa became rigid when a hand grazed her shoulder, not realizing at first that it was only Mark sitting beside her.

"Sorry it took so long. I practically needed a rocket scientist to get the key out of the ignition," he said.

Lisa nodded, not wanting to hear the sound of her own voice. She reached into the rack in the pew before her for the hymnal, hoping she would be able to immerse herself in its lyrics and lose the presence behind her. She felt trapped.

"Don't waste the effort," Christine said knowingly. "He's here."

She turned to Christine, confused, and by the nervousness in her eyes understood that Leslie was behind her. She whirled around and saw Leslie's hands resting on the back of her pew. He was standing behind them, leaning over between Mark's and her shoulder.

"I'm sorry," Leslie said to her and Mark, as if he knew them both equally well.

Mark turned to him, puzzled.

"We all are," Lisa said, barely audible. Christine, she thought, was right: he hadn't changed at all. He may even have looked more attractive than he had at Crosby, because he looked out of place in East Hampton. Too tweedy, too collegiate, adding a gentle layer of vulnerability to his groomed Abercrombie and Fitch facade. It seemed to Lisa to make him more human, more accessible. She noted that his hands were exactly as she had remembered them: long, supple fingers with small patches of blond fur, fingers that had the tanned color of a gardener's, but without that dirty, beaten quality. His nails were perfect ovals, with small sickle moons at the cuticles.

Without turning his head, simply by rolling his eyes to the other side, he looked at Mark and said, "I'm Leslie Nichols. Lisa was a student of mine in Winston. As was Christine here."

"How do you do?" Mark said formally, uneasily. Leslie reached down into the pew for Mark's hand and shook it. Lisa was surprised by how pale Mark's skin was by comparison, and how chubby his fingers were. After squeezing Mark's hand, he glided behind Lisa to Christine.

"You look well, Christine," he whispered, as if administering a sacrament. "But of course I'm sorry to see you under these circumstances."

Christine appeared to shrug him off, but reduced the gesture to a small hiccup with her shoulders.

"Are you going to the reception after the funeral?" he asked her. "At the Graveses' summer place?"

She was silent for a brief moment, and then answered with her most pronounced drawl. "I jus' guess we will. But we sure haven't given it a whole lot of 'think-through.'"

"Please come," he said softly, as if he were the host. "I imagine you all would do the Graveses a world of good."

The organist stopped playing as the Reverend R. Ronald Nigroni and his two assistants entered the church from a back room. They walked to the altar where, standing, they were able to shield the black casket with its silver handles from the congregation. When the organist resumed playing, one of the assistants announced the hymn number, and the more devout groups within the congregation began to sing. She heard Leslie's voice behind her, a practiced tenor, surrounded by many smaller, choked voices. She tried to follow along in the hymnal, but would no sooner find her place among the long rows of numbered lines than the mourners would move on.

Nigroni was a large man with a beard, somewhere in his late forties. He looked to Lisa to be twice the age of his assistants, and twice as heavy. Although he had not struck Lisa as particularly jolly the night before, she had not expected him to speak with such plodding earnestness. He was humorless, and read the psalm by rote.

" 'They have sharpened their tongues like a serpent: adders' poison is under their lips.' "

Mark took Lisa's hand, asking, "All right? You okay?"

"Fine."

" 'Keep me, O Lord, from the hands of the wicked: preserve me from the violent man.' "

"This minister has one bizarre sense of humor," Christine whispered.

Lisa nodded. She sensed Leslie was studying them and wished Christine and Mark would be quiet. She did not want to allow Leslie Nichols any insight into what they thought, how they thought. The fact that Leslie Nichols was there unsettled her.

"Penny Noble was many things to many people," she heard Nigroni begin, and tried to concentrate. "There was Penny Noble, daughter to Michael and Diane Graves, wife to Gordon Noble. There was Penelope Noble, rising young executive at the Dayton-Patterson Company . . ." Lisa's attention wandered back to Leslie Nichols as the litany continued, knowing the vegetable list of Penny Nobles would include no reference to the slighted twenty-one-year-old lover. Out of the corner of her eye she glanced at Christine, and saw Christine was looking back at her. She thought Christine looked as scared and as unhappy as she felt.

When the service ended, four men from the funeral home and two from within the assembled congregation—probably Penny's cousins judging by their age—carried the casket into the rain. Gordon walked directly behind them, appearing as solemn and dignified as the pallbearers, but without their sure step.

Because Leslie was sitting behind them, Lisa, Mark, and Christine left the church before him. The three of them rushed quickly into the station wagon, only Lisa looking back to see what happened to Leslie.

"He still drives that old black and white Mustang," she said to Christine as she climbed into the car.

Mark immediately turned on the heater and then waited for some of the other vehicles to organize themselves behind the family cars.

"So that was Leslie Nichols," he said.

Christine finished pulling on her gloves and leaned forward in the back seat. "He did it, Lis," she said in a monotone. "We both felt it. That slick, seductive fiend did it."

Staring straight ahead Lisa murmured, "Maybe. I'm surprised he's here. It scares me. But I'm not ready to say he did it."

Mark turned to Lisa. "You think Leslie Nichols killed Penny? And Melanie?"

"He might have. He knew them both. He's a link."

"Do you know why he would have killed them?" he asked.

"No. I don't have the foggiest idea. But he has to be a suspect now. He has to be."

Placing his hand firmly on Lisa's knee, Mark continued, "This is important. Could the man who attacked you last night be Leslie Nichols?"

"I guess it could have been, sure."

"Don't guess. Was the build the same? Did the man

who attacked you have the same color eyes as Leslie Nichols?"

"I don't know. About the eyes, that is. And I'm not sure if the man in the ski mask had exactly the same build. Maybe he was as tall, maybe not. But he seemed stockier."

"Okay. Regardless, before we leave for New Hampshire we've got to talk long and hard with that detective. Heckler. Tell him everything you can about your Professor Touchy-Feely."

"He might be at the Graveses'," Lisa said. "I think that's what he told me."

Christine smiled. "We'll nail that slick little sicko, we will." She rubbed Lisa's shoulder, asking, "How's the arm feel, roomie?"

"The arm feels okay," she said, and tried—but failed—to smile back. They might nail him all right, but then again, he might nail them first.

The cemetery was not far from Montauk, a good ten-minute drive from the church. When they arrived at the graveyard, Mark joined the seemingly endless row of cars parked along one of the thin roads crisscrossing the cemetery like veins. The Graveses' plot was a small plateau about thirty yards up a slope.

There were six folding chairs along one side of the trench for the Graveses, the Nobles, Gordon, and Penny's sister, but only Mrs. Graves ignored the rusty drops on the seat and sat down. One of the men from the funeral home tried to keep an umbrella over Mrs. Graves, but gave up when he realized that he was inadvertently forcing her husband away from her side. Lisa also saw Leslie Nichols standing a good twenty yards off to Gordon's right, as if he were afraid to get too close.

Nigroni's voice did not carry well in the rain. He held open his Bible with both hands and attempted to shield the book with his head by looking straight down at it. It seemed to Lisa as if he were speaking directly into the earth.

" 'The Lord is my shepherd; I shall not want.' "

Gordon stared at the minister's black shoes. Occasionally he squeezed Mrs. Graves's shoulder, but she did not seem to notice the gesture. If she noticed anything, Lisa decided, it was the perfectly rectangular pit before her.

" 'Surely goodness and mercy shall follow me all the days of my life and I will dwell in the house of the Lord forever. Amen.' "

"Amen," Christine mumbled, as Gordon threw a lily on the casket.

Slowly the semicircle around the plot began to dissipate. People fell back down the hill like retreating soldiers, slower than a running army, but casting the same nervous glances over their shoulders.

"He doesn't look like a killer, does he," Christine said, nodding at Leslie Nichols.

"I don't think I know what a killer looks like," Lisa responded. "I've never known one."

"Till now."

"Till now," Lisa answered, as Leslie started down the slope to his car.

21

Preserve Me from the Lady's Man

The Graveses' summer home was an immaculate Tudor mansion with mullioned windows and too many chimneys. Behind it was a small creek, and before it a steep hill cut into breasts by the driveway. Mark parked at the top of the hill, remarking sarcastically that the house vaguely resembled the ramshackle cottage in the Catskill Mountains he had bought the year before, except for the fact the Graveses' home was "a million rooms bigger and in a million times better condition."

Inside the home, neighbors and relatives and business associates were wandering from room to room, talking to each other in hushed tones about the meats and cheeses and crudités spread out among the folding card tables.

"Do you see that detective anywhere?" Mark asked Lisa when they were in the front hall.

"No, he doesn't seem to be here yet," she said. "But I'm sure he's coming."

"You want something to drink?"

"I don't think I can. I took one of the tranquilizers the hospital gave me just before we went into the church."

"Well I can drink," Christine said firmly, almost annoyed, and steered the three of them to the makeshift bar in the dining room. There they found a warm, secure cranny away from the scented embraces of plump old women, but still close enough to the front door to see whoever came and went.

Warren Racine, account executive on Dayton-Patterson's beauty soap, Whisper, squeezed Lisa's good arm and kissed her on the cheek. He was standing with a balding, graying, older little man he evidently planned on introducing. The little man looked like a great bowler.

"This has not been one of your better weeks, has it?" Warren asked, trying to smile.

"Nope, sure hasn't," she answered, watching Mark and Christine talk to Gordon across the room.

"Is it even safe for you to be here?"

"I'm just a thrill-seeker, Warren."

"I'm serious! I worry about you. We all worry about you!"

"I'm touched, really and sincerely touched. Who are 'we'?"

"You know. People at the agency."

"Ah, that we."

"Does your arm hurt a lot?"

"Enough. It doesn't feel terrific."

Warren nodded. "Well, I really am scared for you, Lisa. If there's anything I can do—"

"Thank you, but I don't think there's anything anyone can do. Except the police."

"Well, perhaps this man here can at least cheer you up," Warren said. "He tells me he owes you an apology. Lisa Stone, meet Walt Swaggert. Walt, this is Lisa Stone. I gather you two have spoken on the phone."

Lisa turned her full attention to Swaggert, surprised. She knew there were Dayton-Patterson people at the reception, but she had not expected this short man in the checkered suit to be one of them.

"It's good to meet you, Lisa Stone," Swaggert said, smiling. "Warren's right, I owe you an apology. That's why I wanted Warren to introduce us. I want to tell you that I'm sorry I was so abrupt the other day. Things are pretty damn chaotic right now, and I guess I just lost perspective. Took everything too damn seriously."

"I understand," Lisa said, unsure what Swaggert was leading up to.

"D-P has its annual sales meeting in two weeks," Warren explained.

"Well, a sales meeting is no excuse to be rude. So I want to apologize," Swaggert said, extending his hand.

"Apology accepted, but not necessary," Lisa told him, giving him her hand. The moment they shook, she realized he was secretly pressing into her palm a crumpled square of paper no bigger than a quarter.

As soon as possible, Lisa found the Graveses' first-floor powder room and hid there to read the note. With a seven-year-old's penmanship Swaggert had written,

"Call me at home tonight at (203) 555–9715. I hear you're writing an article. Maybe I can help. This is in strictest confidence."

Her article. She wasn't even sure she should or could write that article anymore. A relatively simple piece to clear her friend's name was becoming a nightmare. Suddenly Melanie was dead, and her own life was in jeopardy. And it was beginning to look like she would be wasting her time trying to clear Penny's name in any case, since it was beginning to look like her friend was up to no good after all. She looked at her reflection in the mirror and saw the faint discoloring of her dressing just above the sling. She looked like a battered wife, she decided, pale and beaten and constantly on the verge of tears.

When she left the powder room, she saw that Heckler had arrived. He was standing by the bar with Mark and Christine. He saw her at the same moment she saw him and smiled.

"So I hear you and Christine have solved the mystery," he said lightly as she joined them.

"You mean Leslie Nichols?"

Heckler nodded. "Christine has been giving me the scoop on your old professor. I gather he was quite the lady's man."

"Lady killer, actually," Mark said, sipping a glass of wine.

Lisa wondered if Christine had gone so far as to mention to Heckler the sexual round robin that once went on in Nichols's study. "We're just very surprised to see him here. We hadn't expected it," she said.

"No, I wouldn't have thought so," Heckler agreed. "Christine tells me that neither of you had seen the man since you graduated. Is that correct?"

"That's correct. I know I hadn't seen him before today."

"Since school?"

"Since school."

"Had Penny?"

"Not as far as I know. I tend to doubt it."

"That's exactly what Christine said too," Heckler commented.

"Well, we just got our stories straight before we saw you, I guess," Christine said sarcastically.

Ignoring Christine, Heckler continued, "Tell me about the size of the man who attacked you last night."

"He was big. I've already told you that."

"Was he bigger than your old professor?"

"I don't know. It was dark. Let me see Leslie and I'll tell you."

"I saw him," Christine said. "He's in the kitchen."

"Did he seem bigger than your old professor at the time?" Heckler pressed.

"He seemed wider. Heavier. But I don't believe he was as tall."

"As tall as Leslie . . ."

"Right. He didn't seem as tall as Leslie."

"Then what is it about your attacker that makes you positive it was Professor Nichols?"

Lisa looked at Christine, annoyed: she thought it might have been Leslie, but she wasn't positive. "There was not anything about my attacker that made me think it was Leslie Nichols," she explained. "It's just the fact that Leslie's here. It doesn't make sense, it scares me."

"Why would he have killed Melanie?"

"Maybe because she knew something."

"Such as?"

"I don't know. Maybe something about Penny's death."

"Could Leslie have killed Penny?"

"He could have."

"Okay, why?"

"I don't know!" Lisa answered, raising her voice. "I don't know. All I know is that out of the blue this ghost from the past is here, and suddenly two of my best friends are gone!" Mark quickly went to Lisa and held her, letting her fall against him.

"Can this wait?" Mark asked Heckler.

"Sure," Heckler answered, "it can wait. But look, guys, I'm just doing my job. So please, don't get all bent out of shape here. If you tell me some poor sociology professor from Crosby College is bumping off the alumnae pool, you better have some pretty concrete reasons behind the idea."

"Isn't it enough that he's here?" Christine asked.

"No way. There are a lot of people here."

"But not a lot of people who slept with Penny Noble. Or Melanie Braverman. Or—let's be upfront here—me and Lisa," Christine said, speaking very rapidly. "Look at the facts: years ago, Penny, Melanie, Lisa, and me all lived together. And—at least once—each of us slept with ol' Leslie the Lech. Again, years ago. Now Leslie is back, and Melanie and Penny are dead. What does that tell you?"

Lisa looked down at Mark's shoes, not wanting to concentrate on anything but the wavy white line of rock salt across their tips. They had looked just like that six months earlier at Penny's and Gordon's wedding, the day she and Mark had met.

"Leslie is here to pay his respects to an old girlfriend," Heckler said. "There's no reason to suspect otherwise. Obviously I'll talk to him—I'll talk to anyone at this point—but I haven't seen one piece of evidence that implicates the man in any way."

"Nothing?" Christine asked, incredulous.

"Nothing."

"How is the investigation proceeding?" Mark asked.

"It's moving. Slowly, but it's moving. We now know—we have reason to believe, that is—that the same person who killed Penny also killed Melanie. We got the lab reports back early this afternoon on some clothing fibers found on Melanie's body, and they matched those in Cohn's apartment.''

"Can't you just check those fibers against Leslie Nichols?'' Lisa asked, not looking up.

"Not without a whole lot more substantial evidence than your accusations. We would need a probable cause for a search warrant, and I don't see that it's there.''

"But you will talk to him," Mark said again.

Heckler nodded. "Of course. But frankly, I don't think he's our man.''

"Then who is?'' Christine snapped. "For a cop, you sure don't have a lot of answers!''

Pressing a toothpick between two incisors, Heckler said softly, "You're sure it's Leslie Nichols because he's here out of nowhere. Because you and Lisa and Penny and Melanie once were involved with this man. That's your story. Here's mine: I have an executive from a huge soap company found dead in a pusher's apartment. She definitely was there posing nude, and she might have been there to get a pound cake of cocaine. It's hard to say right now, because on the one hand the package of coke had what might be her name on it, but on the other hand, her purse only had about two hundred bucks in it. A lot of money by most standards, but not nearly enough for the cocaine.''

"Whoever killed her could have taken the money," Mark said.

"Possibility, I agree. Or it was prepaid. Or she was going to pay later. Or someone else paid for it for her. The point is, I don't know. And those are just the questions I have to resolve about Penny Noble. They increase exponentially when you throw in Harris Cohn and Melanie Braverman. Exponentially!''

"Do you plan on talking to the Dayton-Patterson people?'' Lisa asked.

"Sure do.''

"They're here, you know. You could talk to them all right here, right now," she continued.

"I don't think so, Lisa. Not here. Not at this reception. I'll talk to Leslie here, but only because he's probably heading back to Massachusetts today or tomorrow. But I won't talk to your D-P people. Not here."

"Then where?" Christine asked.

Heckler reached into his blazer and pulled out a small note pad. "Monday, two P.M., the office of Maureen Orellono, D-P director of personnel. One by one, everyone Penny Noble worked with will be paraded in to see me."

"That's two days from now," Christine said, disgusted.

"It's soon enough. But you'll probably be safely back in Atlanta by then anyway," Heckler said, "and Lisa here will be safe and secure in New Hampshire."

Lisa heard Heckler, but she wasn't so sure she believed him. She couldn't imagine being "safe and secure" ever again.

Heckler blinked the moment he walked into the kitchen, closing his eyes against the whites and chromes and polished metal of the room. He had never seen a kitchen quite like it, especially in a "summer place." The room looked like a NASA test lab. There was a pasta maker, an espresso pot, and an ice-cream freezer along one counter, a convection oven, a microwave, and a Cuisinart along another. There was a hot smoke and mesquite grill in the center and two sparkling silver vacuum fans along the ceiling, each as big as a small car. And there was still room for a deacon's bench and breakfast table on one side of the room.

He saw Leslie Nichols leaning against the refrigerator, talking to two women he assumed were former students. As soon as he introduced himself, the women scattered.

"I don't always have that effect on people," Heckler said, smiling.

"Just on women then?" Leslie asked.

"Yeah, just on women. Actually, it really is what you might call an occupational hazard. The only time people want cops in their living room is when they're on TV. And the thing is, I'm probably going to have to talk to those two ladies at some point anyway."

"The one with darker hair was Kate Hemmick. English major, but wrote a very sharp essay on the alienation of women in the work place. The blonde is Stacey Penrose. Dyes her hair. Poli-sci major. Couldn't write a paper to save her life, as I recall."

"Very impressive. Do you remember all your students that well?"

"The pretty ones. The smart ones."

"Well, as a matter of fact, I will need to speak to both those women. Do they live in New York?"

"If not in the city itself, then the suburbs somewhere. They both work in Manhattan."

"Know where?"

"No, I'm sorry. They did tell me, but I wasn't paying very close attention."

One of the two old women from the catering service approached Heckler, offering him a cup of coffee, which he declined.

"I imagine it's pretty tough for you to concentrate on much of anything today," Heckler continued.

"Try the last few days, Detective. I heard about Penny on Thursday, and I've been in a bit of a fog ever since."

"When did you get into town?"

"I drove in this morning."

"Long drive, isn't it?"

"Six hours, but all on good roads. The thing is, I stopped for a bite to eat in Westchester—New Rochelle, I think it was—and I bought a paper to read. And to see Melanie dead too, well, that was just devastating."

"I understand you and Penny used to be very close."
Leslie smiled.

"Did you two stay in touch after she graduated?"

"She moved in with me the day after graduation, and stayed through Labor Day. Three months. Does that count?"

"Did you ever see her after that?"

"I called her two years after she graduated. I called her three times, I think. But she wouldn't see me."

"So what brings you here today?"

"Got another one of those?" Leslie asked, referring to Heckler's toothpick.

"I wouldn't have pegged you for a toothpick man," Heckler said, handing him the box like it was a pack of cigarettes.

"I'm not. But it looks good."

"So why did you come here today?" Heckler asked again, genuinely curious.

"I wanted to say good-bye. I did love Penny, Detective. I loved Penny more than I've loved anyone, I think. Is that maudlin?"

"I'm a bad judge of maudlin."

"Because I mean that. I thought about Penny a lot the last five, six years. I thought a lot about 'what if' . . ."

"As I hear it, you hurt her bad."

"I did. I'm not proud of that."

"How come?"

"How come I hurt her?"

Heckler nodded.

"The whole thing seemed to have gotten out of hand. At least at the time it seemed that way. She wasn't pressuring me into marriage—Penny wasn't like that—but the longer we were together, the more marriage seemed inevitable. And I didn't want to be married. I didn't want to be that committed."

"So you sent her home to her parents."

"Essentially, yes."

"Do you get along with the Graveses?"

"You must be joking. They hate me."

"That's what I thought. But the fact you're here . . ."

"I'm here despite the Graveses . . . And it's rather awkward, I must tell you. But I had to come."

"Can I ask you one more serious question?"

"Go ahead."

"Did Penny ever try or use drugs around you?"

Leslie frowned. "Other than grass?"

"Other than grass."

"No. Never. Not once. I don't think the idea ever crossed her mind."

"But she did smoke marijuana?"

"On occasion."

Heckler flipped his toothpick into the trash can. "So tell me, what is the feeling about all this at the college?"

"When I started out this morning about eight, it wasn't an issue."

"Really?"

"Until Melanie was murdered last night, there was no 'Crosby-Slaughter.' There was one murdered woman who happened to have gone to Crosby College."

"How do you think the college will respond now?"

"I can only hope that it won't overreact. But it will. Colleges are reactionary beasts these days."

"So you don't put much stock in 'Crosby-Slaughter'? You don't believe someone is murdering Crosby College alumnae for the hell of it?"

"No, I don't. Crosby alumnae may tend toward the self-important on occasion, but they don't seem particularly deserving of murder."

"Were Penny Noble's and Melanie Braverman's murders coincidence in that case?"

"I don't believe that either. But the connection doesn't have to be Crosby College. They were friends, and had been friends for a decade. I imagine that whatever they were involved in that led to their deaths, they found after college."

Heckler saw that the professor's toothpick was about to split. "You might want to deep-six that," he said, motioning toward the thin strip of wood.

"I will, thank you."

"You like it?"

"Toothpicks?"

"Uh-huh."

"A thoroughly disgusting habit, but I can see their appeal," Leslie said, snapping the toothpick in half with his thumb and forefinger.

"An acquired taste," Heckler added, noticing that a splinter had drawn blood from the professor's thumb.

"Most vices are," Leslie said, staring for a moment at the blood with an intensity Heckler had not realized was there.

22

The Ramblings of an Over-the-Hill Brand Manager

Mark and Lisa had talked about leaving for New Hampshire right after the Graveses' reception. But Christine didn't have a flight back to Atlanta until the next morning, and Lisa wouldn't leave her alone in the city. Besides, she reasoned, it was six-thirty in the evening by the time they returned to Manhattan, and she wasn't sure she could tolerate another six hours on the road. So they agreed they would leave for the Stones' summer house first thing Sunday morning. Lisa also suggested to Christine that she spend the night with them in Mark's apartment, since Gordon was going to spend the night with his family and she would have been alone.

"Oh, goody," Christine had cried sarcastically, "a

slumber party! I'll be sure to bring my new boombox and Wham tapes!" But she had agreed to stay with them.

Lisa phoned Walt Swaggert slightly after seven, with Mark and Christine in the room. She felt somewhat guilty about violating his "strictest confidence" request, but she didn't think she should be hiding things from Mark and Christine at that point. Especially from Christine, since her friend's life was in at least as much jeopardy as her own.

"Hi, Walt, this is Lisa Stone," she said when he answered. "I hope I didn't catch you in the middle of dinner."

"Nope, we eat late in this house, usually around eight-thirty."

"Is now a good time to talk in that case?"

"For me it is. I trust you're alone."

Lisa started to lie, but couldn't. "No, Walt, I'm not. But there are no police here, and no one else is on the line."

"Who's with you?" he asked, annoyed.

"Christine Yarbrough, Penny's and my college roommate. And Mark Scher, a friend of mine."

"What kind of friend?"

"A boyfriend. I'm at his apartment."

"Well, I sure do appreciate your keeping such a tight lid on this."

"Please, Walt, don't be angry. I haven't told the police. And I won't tell the police I spoke to you, if you don't want me to."

Swaggert paused. "I wanted to talk to you because I liked Penny. I liked her a lot. And when somebody told me you were writing an article about her, I thought it was a first-rate idea. I wanted to help."

"You still can."

"But I'm not a confidential source anymore," he said, more frustrated than angry. "I don't think I want to get into this now."

"I *know* I don't want you to," Lisa said. "I know it. But I don't think you have a choice anymore, and I don't think I have a choice anymore."

"What do you mean by that?"

"You cared for Penny, just as I did. So you have to help her, just like me."

"By telling you things you can tell the police . . ."

"Right. But I wouldn't say who my source was, I promise."

Swaggert was silent for a long moment, deciding what to do. Then: "Well. You got a pencil?"

"No. Do I need one?"

"Nah. I'm just stalling. There's nothing exact to write down."

"I didn't think so."

"I can't substantiate any of this with concrete facts," he said, taking a deep breath. "It's not conjecture, but I couldn't prove it either."

"I understand."

"I hope so. And the only reason I'm telling you this is to clear the air a bit about Penny. I have no ax to grind."

"You're stalling again, Walt."

"This is all off the record, right?"

"Right."

"Okay. I told you I'm being driven crazy by the annual sales meeting in two weeks. It's in Fort Lauderdale this year, and it's a nightmare. For me, at least. Because not only do I have to get my own slide presentation together, I'm in charge of the closing video. Plus I still have all my other regular day-to-day responsibilities to stay on top of."

"What does this have to do with Penny?"

"Penny also had a slide presentation to prepare. Two in fact. One on the status of regular, old-fashioned Whisper, and one on the new Whisper Shampoo. It's a brand new product we're introducing."

"Really?"

"Really. Plus, Penny was in charge of entertainment. Entertainment is always the job of the Whisper brand manager. Melissa Hayes was in charge last year, for instance. It's a tradition."

"And?"

"And it's a really tough job. Five hundred salesmen to keep happy, plus their wives. Or husbands, these days. All the D-P brass. The board of directors. Well, it can't hurt to have a little extra help on hand to keep the people happy. Something a little more potent than a piano bar and a washed-up crooner."

"You're telling me that Penny Noble was buying drugs for the sales meeting?"

"I'm not telling you anything. All I'm suggesting is that a successful sales meeting can help a brand manager's career. Get the sales guys all revved up to sell soap, give some key sales reps some extra 'tools' to sell with . . . you get the idea. Make it a good year for the company, and the company will make it a good year for you. They'll thank you, make it worth your while. A little personal investment now can result in very, very big returns come bonus time in eight months."

"That just doesn't sound like Penny. I can't envision her hanging out in alleys looking for drug dealers," Lisa said, baiting Swaggert.

Swaggert laughed just the tiniest bit. "I can't either, I can't either. That's because that's not how it's done. The company—people in the company, I should say—make it as easy as possible. One name, one phone call, one visit. That's it."

"And that one name is—was—Harris Cohn?"

"I wouldn't go around pointing fingers," Swaggert said. "All I'm saying is that Penny Noble did what she did because she had no choice. It was practically in the job description, in my opinion, an unwritten but expected responsibility."

"But you yourself wouldn't go around pointing fingers?"

"Not a prayer. What you're hearing, my girl, are un-substantiated, unproven, unreliable allegations. The ram-blings of an over-the-hill brand manager."

23

"Gender Identification in the New England Pulpit"

Heckler's first thought when he hung up the phone with Lisa Stone was to call Gordon Noble. He wanted a glimpse of Penny's sole and Gordon's joint bank ac-counts. If, as Lisa had suggested, Penny really was pur-chasing drugs from Harris Cohn, it might show on a bank statement or two.

After a moment's consideration, however, he real-ized he had to give Gordon another night of peace. The bank statements could wait until tomorrow. Or Monday even.

Instead he phoned Crosby College, a call triggered more by frustration—a need to do something—than by sound police instincts.

"Good evening," he said to the female operator at the central switchboard, a woman who sounded about eighteen. A student, in all likelihood. "I'm calling to find out the course schedule of Professor Leslie Nichols."

"I can connect you with his office, but I doubt any-one is there. I would suggest you call the registrar's office Monday morning. They open at eight o'clock."

"No, no need to ring the man's office," Heckler said. "Do you have any schedules handy?"

"We really don't print such a thing."

"Do you have catalogs?"

"Yes, of course," the operator said, annoyed. "If you give me your name, I'll have the admissions office send you one."

Heckler started to tell the woman that he was a police officer, but abruptly stopped himself. Telling her he was a detective might intimidate her, perhaps prevent her from telling him anything at all. He might wind up having to wait until Monday morning to find out Leslie's course schedule, when public affairs or public relations or whatever they called it at Crosby College opened. Plus, admitting to the operator that he was a cop interested in Leslie Nichols might seriously damage Nichols's reputation on campus. And as far as Heckler could see, there was just not enough evidence to make Nichols a no-holds-barred, out-of-the-closet murder suspect.

"Look, I don't need to see a whole catalog," Heckler said. "I go to school down the road, at the university. All I need to know is when a couple of classes meet, so I can see if I can sit in for the last few weeks of the semester. Is there a catalog there with you? At the switchboard?"

"Yes, I think so."

"Okay, terrific. It lists courses and professors and when a class meets, right?"

"No, our catalogs don't list courses," the woman said sarcastically. "I think that would be asking an awful lot of a catalog, don't you?"

"I deserved that," Heckler said to appease the operator. "I'm sorry. But can I ask you to look up just one thing for me? Just one thing?"

"That depends."

"All I want you to do is to read to me the name of every sociology course Professor Leslie Nichols is teaching this semester, and the days of the week when they meet. Okay?"

"Is this a joke? Are you with some fraternity?"

"What, is that a difficult thing to do?"

"We must have five or six pages of sociology courses!"

"So how long will it take you to flip through them? A minute?"

"How I spend my Saturday nights. . . ." the woman snorted.

"Please?"

"I'm checking, I'm checking already."

"Thank you."

"All you want is the name of the course and when it meets, right?"

"Right."

"Let's see. Here we go, here's one. 'Courtesies and Careers: Nineteenth-Century Female Intellectuals and the Challenge of Early Feminism.'"

"I'll bet that one packs 'em in."

"It's a two-hour seminar on Monday afternoons, from two to four," the operator said, ignoring his comment.

"Is that all he's teaching?"

"Chill out, will you? I'm still checking. Ah-ha: 'Gender Identification in the New England Pulpit: Sex Roles in the Church from the Half-Way Covenant through the Revolution.'"

"When does that meet?"

"Lecture is Monday, eight-thirty. Seminar is Wednesday, eight-thirty."

"Anything else?"

After a moment the operator said, "Nope. That's his schedule this semester."

"Two classes?"

"Courses. We call them courses here."

"Only two?"

"That seems reasonable to me. He also has his senior thesis students to advise. And his own writing, of course."

"Of course," Heckler mumbled, disappointed. He had hoped to hear that Nichols taught courses all Wednesday, Thursday, and Friday, giving the man an alibi and eliminating him as a suspect.

24

The Only Weapon
She Could Find

Lisa listened to Mark's even breathing, unmoving. It was
3:15 according to Mark's digital clock, 3:10 for the rest of
Manhattan.

She wondered if Christine was asleep in the living
room and decided she probably wasn't. Mark was the
sort who could sleep through anything, anytime, anywhere. Not Christine. Christine was more like herself, a
worrier.

"God knows she has a right to be worried," Lisa
whispered to herself. "God knows I have a right to be
worried."

Fat people usually looked younger than their age,
Lisa thought, but not Christine. Not anymore. She was
aging fast, falling to pieces. Not only was her hair beginning to gray, it looked like it was thinning, the fuzzy
black mound rolling back along her skull like a wind-
wrecked dune. Her elbows and knees were gone, hidden
by rolls of undulating Jell-O. Her bones were probably as
brittle as twigs from too little calcium, and her teeth as
hole-speckled as coral from too many mints, Milanos,
and Milky Way bars. Her skin was a cheerless washed-
out white, her legs a road map of varicose veins, and her
breasts had sagged for years. She was deteriorating, perhaps only slightly more slowly than she would if she
were already dead. She was surrendering to time, eating
like a pig to hide from herself the fact that in reality she
was being tapered off by the second.

Lisa wished they had left for New Hampshire that

night after all. If they had, they would be there by now, probably crawling underneath warm flannel sheets at that very moment. She would be laying in the mahogany four-poster she had slept in every summer as a child, this time with Mark, and watching the moonlit silhouette of Mount Lafayette outside her window. In New Hampshire, her arm might not even hurt.

She wondered where Leslie Nichols was at that moment. Winston? Or had he remained in New York? An image of her former professor trailing a woman down deserted Manhattan streets late at night crossed her mind— his confessed search for the face of fear. For all she knew he was right now on East Eightieth Street, wandering slowly toward Mark's building. . . .

Lisa opened her eyes and forced herself to push the image from her mind. Intimidating a woman on the street—once, many years earlier—and knifing a woman to death were two very different things. It was silly to be scared of Leslie. Especially since it was becoming increasingly clear that Dayton-Patterson was somehow behind Penny's and Melanie's murders.

Regardless, she wished she was in New Hampshire.

Outside Mark's bedroom door, in the living room, she thought she heard a noise. Christine, perhaps, rolling over on Mark's sofa bed. Or stretching. Or tiptoeing into the kitchen for something to eat.

She held her breath for a moment, listening, but the noise was gone. If there had even been a noise. She wasn't sure.

As soon as she exhaled, however, she heard noises again. Movement. Someone crossing the living room floor. Long, measured steps. Careful steps, steps striving for silence. In her mind, she followed them. She envisioned someone walking from the apartment's front door to the sofa bed, someone in a ski mask. She saw Christine asleep, unaware of Melanie's murderer creeping up behind her, over her.

But of course no one was there. Lisa almost whispered the words aloud to herself, but her voice would not respond. She could not bring herself to make one sound, to move even her lips.

But it didn't matter. Because no one was there. It wasn't possible.

And yet someone was moving in the living room, she knew it. Something rustled. She heard it, she was positive, something had rustled. Someone had moved slowly, purposefully across the room, and then something had rustled.

Or been stifled. That was really what the noise was. Someone being stifled, muffled, forced down. She saw Christine asleep, being strangled as she lay alone in the sofa bed. Instead of a long, rusty steak knife, Ski Mask this time had used a pillow.

Lisa considered waking Mark, and might have if she had not been afraid to move. But the fact was she was afraid to move, and she was almost glad, because it would be ridiculous to wake up Mark now. After all, Christine was not really dead, Ski Mask was not really outside their bedroom door. It was all in her mind, it had to be.

As she closed her eyes, however, she heard a door fall shut. Whether it was the front door or the kitchen door she wasn't sure; but this time she knew it was a real noise, a noise as loud and close and horrifying as the pounding of her own heart. Either Christine was up and around, or someone had just come or gone through Mark's front door. But a door had swung shut, that was clear.

So she had to move. Somehow, just because it might not be Christine out there, she had to move. She had to wake Mark and reach for the telephone or find a weapon to defend herself. But she had to move.

She tried to recall Mark's belongings, items he kept in his closet or under his bed that they could use against Ski Mask. Golf clubs, perhaps, or a letter opener. But Mark owned neither. He did have a softball bat that would have been perfect, but she was afraid he had donated it to the office softball team just the other day. She thought there were shoe trees in the closet, and large wooden coat hangers, but neither option struck Lisa as a particularly effective bludgeon against a two-hundred-pound-plus madman.

She strained again to hear activity in the living room, but heard nothing. The room had fallen silent. If someone were there, someone other than Christine, he was standing still, as unwilling to move as herself. Out of the corner of her eye she saw that the clock read 3:35, meaning that she had been lying awake for twenty minutes.

Slowly, with each passing moment of silence, she became less convinced that someone was out there. Someone other than Christine. Whoever had been there was gone. That is, if anyone had been there. It was possible that Christine had simply closed the kitchen door. It wasn't likely, but it was possible.

By 3:45, she was positive that she and Mark and Christine were alone in the apartment.

What she didn't know was whether Christine was alive.

She tried to reassure herself that nothing had happened, that Christine was fine. But she couldn't. She could write off every noise except the last one, a door being closed. She was kidding herself if she believed that Christine had closed a door, she knew it. Someone had been in Mark's apartment, someone had crept inside while she and Mark and Christine slept, and. . . .

And what? Seen Christine on the sofa bed and left? Not likely.

Seen Christine on the sofa bed and . . .

She would not finish the thought.

"Mark!" she whispered urgently, intensely. "Mark!"

Half-asleep, he mumbled. "What?"

"Someone was in the living room!" she told him in a hushed, panicked voice.

Immediately Mark woke up. "Was? Or is?" he asked, pulling her to him.

"Was. I think whoever was there is gone."

"What exactly did you hear?"

"I heard a door close. The front door, I think. I also think I heard someone walking around. But I'm not as sure about that."

"The walking."

"Yes."

"I'll go see," he said, rolling out of bed.

"I'm going with you," Lisa told him, afraid to be alone. She saw he was climbing into the blue jeans he had pulled off the top of his dresser. "Should we bring something? A weapon?"

He looked at her, perplexed, and then nodded. "Yeah, I guess so." He reached into his closet and found the cane he had used two years before, after he had wrecked his knee skiing.

She followed him to his bedroom door, where he stopped. As if he were testing the door for heat, to determine if the next room were on fire, he placed his palms against it. Slowly he ran his hand down to the knob, and even more slowly he turned it, trying, Lisa thought, to open the door noiselessly.

When the latch was released, Mark paused. He turned to Lisa and whispered, "Get behind me. I'm going to pull the door open and run in."

She nodded, and moved behind him, out of his way. She watched him take a breath and hold it, and in the split second before he yanked open the door, recalled Melanie's rolling, dying eyes as she was murdered. And the blood. The blood in Melanie's mouth, on her neck, on the sidewalk. Who knew people had that much blood in them?

Abruptly Mark opened the door, raised his cane, and rushed into the living room. Lisa followed him into the door frame, her eyes adjusting quickly to the different shade of dark in the living room. She looked first at the

Castro, expecting to see that the gallons of ooze that had flowed from Melanie had flowed from Christine. She was sure she would see Christine dead.

Instead she saw nothing. The Castro was empty.

Mark stood immobile, his cane suspended above his head. Lisa slowly followed him into the living room, and stood beside him.

Her eyes circled the room, beginning with the sofa bed and moving clockwise. Past the coffee table with its coasters and catalogs and Hertz bills. Past Christine's opened suitcase. Past the television set, with a pile of newspapers still on it. She saw that the red majolica water pitcher was intact on the dining-room table, as was Mark's Haitian sculpture of a mother rat nursing her young. The room was exactly as it should have been, except that Christine was gone.

Moving sideways like a crab, Mark reached over and turned on the light. At the same instant they both heard the whimpering, but Lisa saw Christine first. She was curled into a ball with her knees against her chest, crying in the corner opposite the front door. In her right hand she was clutching Mark's bread knife, a long thin blade with a serrated edge.

Lisa ran to her and put her good arm around Christine's shoulders. She realized she had never before seen Christine cry. "It's okay, it's okay," Lisa said softly, "we're here. It's okay."

"What happened?" Mark asked.

Christine looked up at Mark and started to answer him, but instead only whimpered again, one feeble, frightened cry.

"It's okay," Lisa murmured again. Gently she pulled away from Christine to see if her friend was hurt. When she didn't appear to be, Lisa took the bread knife away and resumed rocking her.

Mark squatted before the two women and tried to meet Christine's eyes. "Christine," he asked again, "what happened?"

This time Christine would not even look at Mark. She glanced once at Lisa and then collapsed against her shoulder, her body shaking with sad, soft cries. "He was here," she wept, "he was here."

"Who was?" Mark asked.

Christine started to answer, but her words were lost in her tears.

"Who was here?" Mark pressed her. "What man?"

"The man who killed Melanie!" Christine blurted out.

"How do you know that? How do you know it was him?" Mark continued. "Was he in the apartment?"

"No, he couldn't get in," Christine sobbed, "he couldn't get through the chain!"

Lisa looked across the room at the front door and saw the chain lock was still clasped in place. "So you didn't actually see him," she said carefully, softly.

"But who else could it have been?" Christine went on. "Someone tried to break in here while I was right there on that couch! Right there! I heard him! I heard him comin' down the hall, and then I heard him pickin' at the lock. And then he got the door open 'bout an inch before he realized it had a chain on it and closed it again!"

Mark stood up, went to the front door, and pulled it open the inch the chain would allow. "She's right," he said to Lisa. "Someone was here."

Lisa looked at her friend, who continued to quiver against her shoulder, and at the bread knife at their feet. "Oh, sweetie, did you really think that would help?" she asked, alluding to the knife. It looked like a butter knife next to the thing that had killed Melanie.

"It was the only weapon I could find," she said.

Lisa nodded and pulled Christine close. In silence she watched Mark close the front door and walk past them to telephone the police. Though the thermostat in Mark's apartment read seventy-two degrees, she realized suddenly that she was very, very cold.

V

Sunday

25

The Number of Ski Masks Out There

The sun would not rise for another ten minutes, but it was bright enough now in Mark's apartment that Lisa could turn off the living-room lights. It seemed to her to make the room less eerie.

The first two policemen to arrive, the men in uniforms, were still downstairs in the building's basement with Mark, the building's superintendent, and Edgar Burton, leaving Christine and Lisa alone with Richard Heckler. Lisa could tell by the way Christine was sitting on the couch that her nightgown had made her self-conscious about her weight: she was sitting cross-legged in one corner, but she had wrapped a blanket around her like a teepee so that only her head protruded. She wished that Christine had taken the tranquilizer she had offered her earlier.

"I like you people," Heckler said, leaning back against the front door. "But you're bumming me out here, I have to tell you. First of all, you shouldn't even be in this state. You should be in Georgia, and you should be in New Hampshire," he said, motioning toward Christine and Lisa respectively.

"I couldn't get a flight out last night," Christine said irritably.

"And I didn't want to leave Christine alone in New York," Lisa added.

"Then you didn't try hard enough, Christine," Heckler said, chastising her. "You should have called me. I could have gotten you a seat on Delta easier than your hot-shit college can raise money."

"I didn't know you had such clout," Christine mumbled.

"I'm a cop. I can't get people job interviews at Merrill Lynch, but I can get someone in danger out of town."

"Well, you can take it easy now. I'm on a ten-fifteen flight this morning. And soon as Mark drops me off at the airport, he and Lisa are going straight to New Hampshire."

"That does make me happy, don't get me wrong," Heckler said. "Look, I don't want to bust your chops here. It's just that this whole thing could have been avoided."

"Look at the bright side," Lisa said lightly, "maybe your friends in the basement will find another clue now."

"I also have a lot more questions."

"Such as?" Lisa asked.

Heckler sat down on the couch, opposite Christine. "Let's just talk in the abstract here for a second. Let's take the first murders, Penny Noble and Harris Cohn. Those were sloppy, messy murders. The work of a rank amateur, a minor-league killer. Let's take the second murder, Melanie Braverman: that was messy, but it wasn't sloppy. That was a well-planned execution. It might have been the work of an amateur, but I doubt it. My guess is pro. Now let's take tonight, the intruder here: that man was absolutely, positively an expert in his field. A definite, certified professional."

"What makes you say that?" Christine asked.

Heckler smiled and put a toothpick in his mouth. "A man gets in and out of a building with a twenty-four-hour doorman without being seen, picks a dead-bolt lock, and you ask me if he's a pro? Come on, Christine, give the guy who was here tonight his due. He was a pro."

"Couldn't he have just come in through the basement?" Lisa asked.

"You don't know much about this building, do you?"

Lisa shrugged. "Guess not."

"Bet it's like my high-rise in Atlanta, eh Detective?" Christine asked.

"No elevator to the basement after eight?" Heckler asked.

"Eight? Now that's paranoid. In my building, you can go to the basement as late as eleven," Christine told him.

Heckler turned to Lisa and explained, "As a defense against burglary, you can't call for the elevator in this building from the basement after eight o'clock at night. That's why your intruder couldn't have 'just come in through the basement.' He could have escaped out the basement, however, that's possible. You can take the elevator down to the basement after eight o'clock and get out. You just can't get back in after the doors close."

"So how do you think he got in?" Lisa wondered.

"We won't know for sure until the boys are done downstairs, and my man Edgar has done his thing in the lab. My guess is that he came in through the front door at either six forty-five P.M. or eleven ten P.M., when the doorman went to the bathroom, and then hung out in a back stairway until three twenty this morning."

"And then he escaped through the basement?"

"Perhaps. A pro would figure it out."

"So what are you gettin' at with all this stuff about pros and amateurs?" Christine asked Heckler. "You tellin' us you think there's more than one killer out there?"

"Maybe. Or maybe he's just getting better with practice," Heckler said thoughtfully.

"I don't think that's real funny," Christine said.

"Wasn't meant to be."

"Because I was scared," she went on, "I was

scareder 'n I've ever been in my life. You don't know what it's like to hear someone on the other side of a door screwin' around with the lock, someone you know wants to kill you."

"I appreciate that," Heckler said.

"I hope you do, Detective. I sure as shit hope you do. Because I was closer to death last night than I wanna be for a good long time."

Lisa came around the back of the couch and gently rubbed the back of Christine's neck. "Seriously, do you think there's more than one person involved?" she asked the detective.

"At this point, I wouldn't worry about the number of Ski Masks out there," Heckler answered. "I'd just get the hell out of town."

26

Sunday Morning in the Suburbs

Heckler reached Walt Swaggert's Connecticut home a few minutes before eight o'clock and decided that as a concession to civility, he would let Swaggert sleep until eight-thirty. After all, it was Sunday morning.

The only people awake in the quiet residential neighborhood were two small boys playing whiffle ball in their driveway. Brothers, Heckler decided, brothers. It wasn't so much that they looked alike, as the way the older child was tolerant of the younger one's woeful inability to swing a hollow plastic bat. Heckler parked his silver Toyota across the street from Swaggert's home and turned his rearview mirror so that he could watch the whiffle ball game down the street. It was the nicest thing he had seen all week.

A little girl with sleepy brown hair and a dead Smurf answered the door. She might have been seven.

"Hello, is your dad home?" Heckler asked quickly, awkwardly. He was never very good at talking to children.

The little girl nodded yes, but didn't leave the doorway. Heckler noticed that the Smurf had only one eye, confirmation that the creature had seen better days.

"Can I see him? Your dad?"

"He's asleep."

"Could you wake him up?"

Something in Heckler's tone, its edge or its intensity, struck a chord in the child, and she ran down the hall and up the stairs, screaming for her father. While she was gone, Heckler surveyed the house and was impressed. It was a fairly cold, gray-shingled colonial on the outside, but the inside was warm and comfortable. It felt lived-in, unaffected. It smelled of fireplace.

Swaggert and his wife appeared at the top of the stairs a few moments later, Swaggert in a pair of baggy paisley pajamas, his wife in a red Lanz bathrobe. Heckler wondered briefly if the little girl was adopted: the Swaggerts looked too wrinkled to have a seven-year-old daughter. Then again, maybe they just looked wrinkled because it was early; maybe they got better as the day went on.

"Can I help you?" Swaggert asked, his voice a combination of fear and defiance.

"I hope so. My name is Richard Heckler, I'm a detective with the New York City police department."

Swaggert's wife squawked unhappily. She immediately put her hand over her mouth.

"I'm Walt Swaggert, and this is my wife, Nora. This

couldn't wait until Monday? I'm supposed to see you people tomorrow anyway."

"No, it couldn't wait. Lisa Stone and Christine Yarbrough had a visitor last night, and I would like to talk to you about him. I promise you, I had no more desire to drive out here this morning than you have to talk to me now. In any case, accept my apologies."

"Would you like some coffee, Mr.—Detective— Heckler?" Nora Swaggert asked.

"That would be nice, if it isn't any trouble." Heckler saw the little girl hiding behind the half-open kitchen door.

"No, it's no trouble," Swaggert said. "I could use some myself. Why don't you follow me into the family room."

In the Swaggerts' home, the family room could not have been more aptly named. It struck Heckler as a tribute to Walter and Nora's fertility. Lining the wood-paneled walls were photographs of at least six different children, ranging in age from the little girl with the Smurf to two apparent college graduates. There were boys in Little League, girls in scouting, big kids on horseback, and little kids in long johns; there were family portraits posed by Christmas trees, taken by barbecues, and snapped beside snowmen. There were Walt and his sons in bowling shirts and Nora and her daughters in tennis skirts. And in all the pictures, all the children were smiling. This, Heckler thought to himself, was one happy family. Definitely not the sort of group that had cops in their family room on a regular basis.

The idea of interrogating Swaggert depressed Heckler. It was one thing to harass the Rudy Cohns and Mindy Lombardos of the world, but Walt and Nora Swaggert? This nice suburban couple? What had they done to deserve me, Heckler asked himself. He started to feel guilty about waking them up on a Sunday morning, and had to remind himself why he was there: Penny Noble. Melanie Braverman. Even Harris Cohn. As nice a man as Swaggert probably was, he knew more about Penny Noble—and perhaps Harris Cohn—then he was letting on. It was time he talked.

"So what's all this about a visitor?" Swaggert asked, motioning for Heckler to sit in the large easy chair while he fell on a corner of the couch. "Is Lisa all right?"

"She's fine. So is her friend, Christine Yarbrough. But last night, at approximately three-twenty A.M., someone snuck into the building where Lisa and Christine were staying and tried to break into their apartment. Fortunately, he didn't make it."

"Did you catch the man?"

"No, he got away."

"Well, my family can tell you flat out that I was snoring my butt off upstairs at three-twenty this morning."

"It never crossed my mind that you were anywhere else."

"Then why are you here now?"

"Because I think you know who dropped by Lisa and Christine's slumber party last night."

"What makes you think that?"

Heckler leaned forward in the easy chair and put his hands on his knees. "Because at five after seven last night, Lisa Stone phoned you to get your help with her article on Penny Noble. You told her that you thought it was possible Penny was scoring dope from Harris Cohn to distribute at the annual sales meeting, perhaps with the knowledge and tacit permission of senior Dayton-Patterson executives."

"So?"

"Lisa Stone wasn't home last night, and not many people knew where she was. You were one of the few who did."

"I have no idea where Lisa Stone was last night, Detective, or what she did. She called me, remember?"

"She says she told you she was at her boyfriend's apartment."

"Whose name I promise you I don't know."

"She says she told you his name."

"It seems to me it's my word against hers. And clearly this woman does not keep her word. She told me I'd remain an unnamed source. Evidently, I haven't."

"Lisa Stone gave me your name at five A.M. this morning. And the only reason she gave it to me was because of her nocturnal guest. She wouldn't have revealed your name if someone hadn't tried to break into the apartment. Trust me on that. Trust her."

"I still don't see what this has to do with me."

"Come on, Walt, give me a break. Would the connection be more apparent if we went down to the station to talk about it? In Manhattan?"

Swaggert's wife returned to the living room and placed the coffee tray on the small table beside the easy chair, and then sat down on the couch beside her husband.

"Look, Walt," Heckler continued, softening his tone for the benefit of the man's wife, "I don't mean to be an arm-breaker. That's not my style. And I don't believe you're a bad guy, not for a second. But I do believe you know more than you've let on. With all that out on the table, let's talk. Okay?" He noticed that Nora's hand was shaking when she poured their coffee.

"Ask whatever you like, Detective," Swaggert said. Heckler couldn't tell if he was resigned or disgusted or both.

"Who told Penny Noble it was her responsibility to buy dope?" he asked.

"I doubt anyone told her it was her responsibility."

"Where did she get the idea?"

"Probably from another brand manager."

"Who?"

"I don't know."

"Who do you think?"

"It could have been any one of a dozen people."

"I want a name."

"I can't do that, it would just be speculation."

"Then speculate."

"That wouldn't be fair."

"I don't care about fair!" Heckler said, raising his voice. "It isn't fair that the woman is dead now, is it? It isn't fair that Harris Cohn is dead either, is it? Or Melanie Braverman? I didn't drive out here for fair, Walt, I drove out here for names. And when I drive back into the city, I promise you I'll either have names or I'll have you. Understand?"

"Perfectly. But Detective—"

"Ed Simmonds," Nora blurted out. "Ed Simmonds must have known."

Swaggert looked quickly at his wife, more disappointed than angry, and then down at the floor.

Heckler tried to recall which brand Simmonds ran, but momentarily drew a blank. Then it hit him. Simmonds wasn't a brand manager, he was a corporate vice president. Vice president of marketing, in fact. He had not been just Penny Noble's boss, he had been Penny's boss's boss.

"Is that true?" he asked Swaggert.

"I don't know if Ed suggested it. But he probably knew all right," Swaggert said softly, in almost a whisper.

"Why is that? Did D-P actually give her the money to buy drugs?"

"No, they wouldn't do that. Too obvious a paper trail. Too many people would have to know."

"Then why? Why should he have known?"

When Swaggert hesitated, his wife jumped in. "Because Ed Simmonds and Penny Noble used to be having an affair," Nora said. "When Penny Noble was still Penny Graves. They go back to the days when Penny used to work for Walt."

"How many years?"

"Let's see," Swaggert began, "she started at D-P fresh out of Columbia, little under three years ago. She was assigned to me on Sunshine, as my assistant. It would have been around June or July. June, I think. And I would say she and Ed were an item until she met the guy she married. Gordon. So I guess a little more than a year. But I'm guessing here, Detective, don't misunderstand me. Penny and I were friends, but we weren't so close we talked about things like that. I just know what I know from the grapevine."

"But they stayed good friends even after they broke up, isn't that right?" Nora asked her husband.

"That's right," Swaggert nodded. "They were pretty damn tight. We all knew that."

"Is Ed Simmonds married?"

"Sure. Has a couple kids too."

"Why did they break up? Ed Simmonds and Penny?"

"I guess because Penny met a guy she loved who would marry her."

"Ed Simmonds was not about to marry her, I gather."

Nora put her hand on Swaggert's knee, a signal that she wanted to speak. "Ed Simmonds is the kind of man who has affairs," she said, "not the kind of man who leaves his wife. Ever."

"Look, that isn't the point," Swaggert said quickly, more to his wife than to Heckler. "I think Ed might have known what Penny was doing, I really do. But not because he once had an affair with Penny."

"Then why?" Heckler asked again.

"Because he decides on the bonuses, Detective, he decides what the annual, year-end bonus for each brand manager will be."

"What exactly does that mean, Walt?"

"We get bonuses on top of our salaries. That bonus is based on a lot of things. What kind of year the company has as a whole. How our own brand does. How we do against our own personal goals. That sort of thing."

"And?"

"And no two brand managers get the same bonus.

It's not an across-the-board kind of thing. And it's Ed Simmonds's responsibility to decide our bonuses."

"And Penny would have gotten a larger bonus because she purchased cocaine for the sales meeting?"

"Well, she would have gotten paid back, that's for sure."

"Who dropped in on Lisa Stone and Christine Yarbrough last night, any ideas?"

"No, I really don't know. I honestly, truly don't know."

"You didn't tell anyone you had spoken to Lisa Stone?"

"Not a soul."

Heckler nodded and stood up to leave. Over Nora's shoulder he saw the little girl hovering in the hallway. She had her mother's eyes, he decided, wide and scared and unhappy.

27

What Nancy Drew Knew

Lisa pressed an extra sweater flat in her overnight bag with her right arm, frustrated by the uselessness of her left, and then zipped the bag shut. It would be chilly in New Hampshire this time of year, especially since it had been such a cold, wet spring. But it would also be very pretty, since the first ribbons of green and yellow would be forming just below the white tips of the White Mountains. She saw by the clock on Mark's bureau that it was almost eight-thirty, meaning that because of her injury, it had taken her almost thirty minutes to pack in one small bag the few pieces of clothing she had at Mark's.

"Honest, Lis, Mark doesn't have to drive me out to the airport," Christine said, sprawled across Mark's bed. "It's real sweet of him, but he doesn't have to."

"He wants to," Lisa told her, "he doesn't mind at all." She lifted the overnight bag to see how heavy it was, and satisfied she could manage it, went on, "Of course, if my father doesn't get here with the car soon, you might be better off taking a cab. It might be the only way you'll make your plane."

"Is he really bringing in the Catalina?"

"Yes he is."

"You know, when I first saw that car seven, eight years ago, I never thought it would make it to your senior year. I never told you that, but I thought that car was a hurtin' puppy even then."

"Guess you were wrong. That Catalina has been my dad's station car for six years now. Since I graduated."

"Are you sure it will get to New Hampshire?"

Lisa sat down on the bed beside Christine and leaned against the headboard. "That car has driven from New York to New Hampshire and from Massachusetts to New Hampshire for twenty years. I could fall asleep at the wheel, and it would steer its way there."

Outside in the living room they heard Mark speaking on the phone with an associate in his law firm. Since he planned on spending the next week in New Hampshire with Lisa, he needed to tie up a number of loose ends at the office.

"What do people in your agency think of you leaving?" Christine asked.

"I only spoke to Jack O'Donnell. He's the account director."

"And?"

"And he's glad I'm leaving. But I have to admit, I got the feeling that the idea I won't be talking to D-P people for a while made him happier than the fact I'll be safer in New Hampshire. He just wants me out of here."

"What do you mean by that?"

"I don't know. Maybe I'm imagining it."

"Nah, you're not the type who sees demons in the air. You're not southern enough."

"Do you think it's possible Penny was buying cocaine? For business?"

"Oh man, Lis, that corporate scene is your deal, not mine. I'm the corporate dropout, remember?"

"Wager a guess."

"If I had to guess, I'd guess it was true. I'd guess it's possible ol' Penny was having herself a little shoppin' spree on the company. Probably wasn't the first time, either, Lis, if she knew 'bout Harris Cohn's photography business too."

"The nude pictures."

"Yeah, the nude pictures."

Lisa found herself hugging a pillow, and put it down. "You don't think she was set up, do you?"

"Like how?"

"I don't know that either. It's just that everyone at Dayton-Patterson is so hush-hush about this. I have to wonder. And look at last night: no one knew where we were but Walt Swaggert."

"I guess that's true," Christine said, and then smiled. "'Course I'm biased. I'm convinced everyone in big business is corrupt. Except you."

"I would hardly classify my job as part of big business."

"Seems to me O-M-R and Pilgrim Paper are pretty damn big."

"All I do is help make ads."

Christine was silent for a long moment, staring out the window. She then rolled over and asked quietly, "Do you think there will ever be a day again when I'm not scared?"

"Of course there will be," Lisa answered, trying to comfort Christine. "Once they catch whoever's doing this, there won't be anything to be scared of."

Christine looked intently at Lisa, and then said, "I'm supposed to be one tough bitch, but I got a feelin' you're toughin' this one out better 'n me."

"Don't get me wrong, I'm scared too—"

"Not like I am," Christine insisted, cutting her off. "You don't seem to jump every time the phone rings. I do. You don't seem to be afraid to go down to the deli to get a turkey sandwich, or across the street to the newsstand to get an idiot magazine. I am. Jeez, Lisa, I'm convinced Leslie Nichols is behind every door I open right now, or one of your corporate arm-breakers is standing outside every goddamn building! That's how scared I am!"

"It would take a lot more than a turkey sandwich to get me outside alone," Lisa said. She saw her friend was shivering slightly.

"Any way you look at it, I win the Chicken Bowl. It's that simple. I'm just glad to be gettin' out of town with my skin."

Lisa shrugged. "In some ways, I hate leaving now. I really do. There's so much I don't know."

"What do you think, if you stayed here you'd figure it all out yourself?"

Lisa tried to smile. "Sure, me and Nancy Drew."

"Well, I got to tell you, Heckler doesn't need her. Or you. He knows everything we know and more."

"Think so?"

"Oh God, I hope so. Because Lisa—no offense here—we don't know squat."

Lisa said good-bye to Christine on the street outside of Mark's building while Mark double-parked the Catalina. Lisa briefly considered going with Christine to La Guardia Airport and saying good-bye to her there, but Mark insisted she stay in the city and relax. After all she had been through, he said, he saw no reason for her to sit in traffic for two hours.

"You plan on laying low in Atlanta, right?" Lisa

asked. Christine was gnawing at the corner of a dark chocolate Milky Way.

"I won't do anything stupid, I promise. Will you do the same?"

"Lay low?"

"And not be stupid, woman! Cut out the Nancy Drew shit!" Christine told her, half-smiling. She was un-aware of the small black chocolate slivers on her upper lip.

"I'll be good. I'll be careful."

"Promise?"

"Promise."

Christine wrapped her arms around Lisa's shoulders in such a way that Lisa heard the candy bar wrapper crin-kling loudly beside her ear. It sounded like a burning newspaper. "I'll miss you," she whispered, and Lisa could tell by the way her friend was breathing that she was beginning to tear.

"I'll miss you too," Lisa said. She shut her eyes and tried not to cry, but it didn't work. Her last image of Christine that morning, a lumbering whopper of a woman with a Milky Way, was softened for Lisa by a nylonlike wave of tears.

28

A Statue of Liberty for the Catskills

Mark seemed to enjoy driving the Catalina, Lisa thought; he seemed to like the car as much as she did. It was an ungainly automobile, big and undisciplined and overcon-fident, but Lisa was more comfortable being held in its primitive frame than she was when hurtled forward by new, more civilized models: after all, no '66 Catalina ever ran out of gas, because the tank held twenty gallons; no one ever died in a '66 Catalina fender bender, because the fender was so far away; and no flat ever stranded a '66 Catalina, because the trunk could hold two spares. This '66 Catalina was blue, almost the same blue as Lisa's eyes. That's why she had picked it out when she was five years old, over twenty years ago, when her father had asked her to choose a car. He had been sure she would pick the red Thunderbird, giving him an excuse to bring home a sports car instead of a family car.

The trip was proving easier than Lisa had expected. It was just after noon, and they were already north of Bridgeport. If they didn't stop, they would be at the Stones' summer home in New Hampshire by five o'clock. This would be the first time Lisa had been there in almost two years, and the first time she had been there in any month other than August since college. It would be the first time Mark had ever been there.

Although they would be there in five hours if they drove straight through, she knew they would stop. She would insist. The Howard Johnson's near Springfield, Vermont, the only exit for twenty miles on that stretch of highway, would be too inviting. She decided she would allow themselves thirty minutes for a late lunch (in her case, coffee and an English muffin) when they got there, which should be a little before three-thirty.

The cars that kept company with the Catalina became more distantly spaced as they drove into New England. The last time there had been anything that even vaguely resembled traffic was just north of Stamford, and even then the cars flowed steadily at forty miles an hour. Lisa reached through the pile of Mark's clothes that smothered the front seat to turn on the car radio for the first time that afternoon. She was not sure whether she was doing it to help stay awake—suddenly she was very tired—or because she was scared. She and Mark had been almost completely silent since they had passed the

exit for her parents' home in Bronxville: the initial excitement they both had felt upon escaping Manhattan had
worn off, leaving them both merely nervous and exhausted.

Alternately spinning the radio dial and pushing the
rectangular buttons, Lisa found a talk show, a rock station broadcasting from a university, and the news twice.
She settled for college rock, though she was concerned
that some twenty-two-year-old disc jockey would make
her feel old. She knew after only a few songs, however,
that her fears were unfounded: she was familiar with everything he played, meaning either that the deejay himself was a relic, or that college pop had changed little in
six years. She was sure it was the latter that was true.

As they approached New Haven, just south of the
bridge where the Merritt Parkway became the Wilbur
Cross, Mark reached over with his right hand and ca-
ressed Lisa's thigh. "Okay?" he asked.

She nodded. "How about you?"

After a long pause, he said slowly, "I'm concerned."
He had said it deliberately, after taking a deep breath.

"I should hope so."

"I'm concerned about our going to New Hampshire," he continued, shaking his head. "I'm not so sure
it's the right thing to do."

Surprised, Lisa turned toward him in the seat. "You
can't be serious. This is a straight line, isn't it?"

"No, I'm completely serious. On the way to the airport, Christine mentioned that you and your roommates
used to go to New Hampshire pretty often when you
were at Crosby. You and Penny, or you and Christine, or
you and Melanie. Whatever."

"So?"

"So if Penny knew about your place in Sugar Hill, so
did Leslie Nichols. And Gordon Noble."

For a brief moment Lisa stared at Mark, uncom-
prehending. And then she understood. "Oh no, Mark,"
she said, raising her voice irrationally, "no, that's not

possible. They aren't there, neither of them, they are not there." As she spoke she imagined Leslie Nichols greeting her from the bay windows in the dining room, holding in his hand the carving knife that had butchered Melanie Braverman; she envisioned Gordon Noble leaning against the fireplace in the living room, a blue and orange ski mask on the floor by his feet. She began to feel nauseous and tried instinctively to combat the feeling by swallowing hard. "They aren't there, Mark," she said again, "it just wouldn't be fair!"

"I don't think 'fair' is an issue here," he said softly, trying to keep his voice calm.

"Even if one of them did know about Sugar Hill, that doesn't mean he would think to go there now. Or would know how to find the place, if he did think of it . . ."

Mark slowed the car and pulled off to the side of the road, reminding Lisa of her Friday night with Gordon. "Sugar Hill has never sounded to me like a big, impersonal metropolis," he said as the car bounced to a stop. "I'm sure both Leslie Nichols and Gordon Noble have the brain power to track down the Stones' ancestral homestead in no time at all."

"But why would they even think to go there now?"

Mark shrugged, and then wrapped his arms around Lisa's shoulders and pulled her toward him. "I'm not sure they would think of it," he said gently. "The fact is, they probably wouldn't. But what if? What if on the outside chance Leslie Nichols really did murder Penny Noble and Melanie Braverman, and is now after you? What if he did think to look for you in Sugar Hill?"

Lisa stared back at him, waiting.

"We would be in real big trouble, that's what. We would be all alone in an oversize house on top of an oversize foothill, with an oversize killer wandering around the basement."

"What are you suggesting? Do you think we were better off in Manhattan?"

"Good God, no, that wouldn't be very smart either."

"Then what?"

"Chippewa Lake," Mark answered, referring to the small lake in the middle of the Catskill Mountains on which he had bought a tired—but he had always said comfortable—summer home.

"You want us to go to Chippewa Lake?" she asked, pulling away from him. "Instead of Sugar Hill?"

Mark nodded. "I think so. This has been in the back of my mind since I drove Christine to the airport. The more Christine and I talked about Sugar Hill, the more uncomfortable I got."

"Do you really believe we'd be safer there? At your place?"

"I sure do," he said, his voice an odd combination of determination and an almost mock sincerity. It had a tone to it Lisa had never heard before, and it made her just the slightest bit uncomfortable. "After all, absolutely no one would have any idea where to find us. Not Nichols, not Noble, not Dayton-Patterson. No one."

"Except the police."

"Except the police. Obviously we would tell Heckler where we were."

Lisa watched the cars speed by, Volvos and BMWs and little Dodge Colts, and wished she were in any of them. This time of the day, most cars seemed to be filled with happy blond families, immaculately dressed couples in country-club clothes traveling to Stratford or Wallingford or New Haven. Their decisions probably revolved around tee-off times, brunch plans, or whether to get their cars washed. They certainly didn't waste any effort wondering where best to hide from a murderer.

"But I wanted you to see Sugar Hill," she said finally, her voice little more than a whisper. She knew her disappointment was ludicrous, but she couldn't help it: she really *did* want Mark to see Sugar Hill.

"I know you did," he told her, taking her hand and rubbing it. "And some day I will see it. Memorial Day, maybe, or this summer. We'll go away for a long weekend and just relax. But right now I think we're better off going to Chippewa Lake."

"How far is it from New York City?"

"About two hours."

"That's not very far."

"But the point is, no one would know we were there."

She put her head back against the headrest and closed her eyes: there again was Gordon Noble by the Stones' fireplace, his eyes as cold and unfeeling as they had seemed Friday afternoon at his apartment. "If you think Chippewa Lake is our best bet, I won't argue with you," she murmured. "I'll trust your judgment."

"I know we're doing the right thing," he said confidently, squeezing her hand so hard that it hurt.

It was just west of Poughkeepsie that they saw the Howard Johnson's, its orange roof and blue neon sign a beacon, a signal, an invitation to all wayward travelers and strays. This particular Howard Johnson's did not look to Lisa as well maintained as what she viewed as the pride of the chain in Springfield, Vermont, but it was still Howard Jonhson's: a Statue of Liberty for the Catskills, accepting into its warm booths that smelled of maple syrup the highway's tired and poor and huddled masses yearning to stretch their legs.

In the restaurant with them sat a family in a booth, a tired mother and father and three messy children crying for ice cream. The children were somewhere between four and ten, and traveling clearly disagreed with them. They were cranky, as were their parents, and the five of them snapped and hissed at each other like kittens from separate litters. There was also a pair of women at the far end of the counter, in all likelihood employees recently off a 6:00 A.M. to 2:00 P.M. shift at some tired little shoe factory or paper mill. They might have been mother and daughter, but the resemblance might also have stemmed from their eyeglasses. They had identical tortoise-shell frames, with rims as wide and round as their coffee cup saucers.

They were served coffee by a teenage girl, maybe sixteen years old. Lisa wondered briefly why she wasn't in school, and then noticed the thin wedding band on her finger.

"How is your arm?" Mark asked, sipping his coffee.

"It was beginning to hurt, so I took a pill when I was in the ladies' room."

He nodded.

"Are you going to call Heckler from here?" she asked.

"I probably should. I had the phone disconnected for the winter, so I won't be able to call from the house." He reached into his wallet and removed his AT & T calling card, and then took one last sip of his coffee. "I love Ho-Jo coffee," he said, standing.

"Would you ask Heckler to tell my parents where we're going? And why?"

"Absolutely. Unless you want to call them yourself."

"No, I don't feel up to that."

He kissed her forehead and wandered across the restaurant to the pay phone. Watching him call Heckler, she became more comfortable with the idea of going to Chippewa Lake. It was an abrupt change of plan, but it wasn't an illogical one: Mark was right, they couldn't be too careful. When he returned, she asked him whether he had spoken to Heckler directly.

"Yeah. I gather he had dropped by the precinct to look over the report on last night."

"Does he like the idea of our going to Chippewa Lake?"

"Absolutely," Mark answered. "He thought it was great."

"And he's going to call my mom?"

"Yes."

"So everything will be all right?"

"Everything's fine," he said, smiling.

She reached across her body and ran a finger along his thigh. He really was very good, and he really did take very good care of her. She considered again telling him that she loved him, as she had in the hospital, but was afraid to speak. She did not want him to hear the tremor in her voice. It would sound, at least to her, as if she loved him only because she was afraid—afraid of Gordon Noble, or Leslie Nichols, or some faceless Dayton-Patterson thug. Afraid of death, of dying with no one to help her.

Wasn't that, after all, why so many people married? Because they were afraid of dying alone?

Heckler got the news—that Mark Scher was going to drag Lisa Stone to some obscure lake she had never seen before in the ass end of the Catskills—from the sergeant who took the message. He got to the station about ten minutes after Mark called.

Although he couldn't argue with the rationale Mark had given the sergeant—nobody would know where he and Lisa were—it didn't seem fair to him to put Lisa in an unfamiliar setting. That was why he loved the idea of Sugar Hill: not only was it far away, it was clearly a place where Lisa could relax and catch her breath. It was a home for her, a hill filled with a lifetime of happy memories. Things that might take her mind off the murder of her friends.

What really irritated Heckler, however, was the fact that Lisa was virtually unreachable on Chippewa Lake: Mark had told the sergeant that his phone was disconnected.

Frustrated, he tried to find Chippewa Lake on three different maps, but evidently it was too small. It figured. He told himself that this was the last time he would drop by the station house on a Sunday afternoon when he wasn't on duty.

By the time Mark and Lisa left Howard Johnson's, it was past two-thirty. For the next hour and a half they

drove through small towns and villages, each looking for-
lorn and unappreciated, burned out in the afternoon sun.
The Montgomery Ward in Evanston, displaying print
housecoats on chipped mannequins in its front windows.
The old independent grocery store in Warbridge, its
muddy parking lot in desperate need of asphalt. The li-
quor store in Dunville, its neon road sign illuminating
only the letters l and r. The towns caught Lisa off guard:
this was a far cry from the New Hampshire she planned
on seeing, the hills where once she had fantasized about
raising children on blueberries and maple spread, and
writing for the local newspaper.

She was relieved when they finally reached the
gravel road around Chippewa Lake, able to put the tired
little towns behind them for the day. The road gradually
took them to a short driveway, at the end of which
loomed Mark's summer house.

Or "lurked," Lisa thought to herself. Some houses
loom, some sit; Mark's lurked. It wasn't proud enough or
big enough to loom; so instead it squatted at the end of
the driveway, lurking out of sight from the cars that
drove by on the gravel road. The house had two stories,
but the second story windows were all the size of paper-
back books. There was a large picture window in one
room on the first floor, but all it appeared to look out on
was the driveway. The outside walls were mustard
yellow, with paint peeling across the front in great lep-
rous splotches. The window screens were ripped. And
the roof, a crazy quilt of slate and tin and tar, looked to
Lisa about as watertight as a colander. She knew it was
the sort of place that was dark inside, even at midday.

"From the front it doesn't look like much," Mark
said apologetically. "I'll probably be fixing it up for the
next hundred years. But wait till you see the back. I have
a beautiful view of the lake, and the dock is in tiptop
shape."

"But it's too cold to swim," Lisa answered distantly.

"Well, yes. But it's still pretty down there."

Lisa continued to stare, ignoring Mark. If she were in Sugar Hill that very second, she would see freshly painted white walls catching the last rays of sun like a mirror. She would see a tremendous porch facing the Presidential Range, Mount Lafayette a light blue shadow in the distant haze.

Instead, she saw a lurking, squatting, gloomy little cavern.

"What do you think, should we unpack in the morning?" Mark asked.

"What?"

"I said, do you think we should unpack in the morning?"

Unpack. To unpack would suggest they were staying. Indefinitely. "That's a good idea," Lisa answered, not wanting to hurt Mark's feelings by commenting on the house, but not wanting to stay in it either. "We can unpack some other time. Why don't we go buy some groceries first?"

Around four-thirty, as he was preparing to leave the station house for the day, Heckler thought he should call Christine Yarbrough in Atlanta, to make sure she had arrived there safely. It was a courtesy in his eyes really, nothing more.

When all he got was her answering machine, however, he became concerned and decided to phone Delta Airlines. A very sweet woman with a very pronounced southern accent took his call, the sort of airline service representative who can make a wind sheer sound routine. As far as she was concerned, it was just the best news possible this side of Chattanooga that there was no record of a Christine Yarbrough making it onto the 10:15 flight to Atlanta.

VI
Monday

29

The Forests Filled
with Demons

Lisa toweled herself dry after her bath, gently patting her left arm. The sky was overcast, and there was a thick fog on the lake—so thick that she was unable to see the other side a scant half-mile away. The daffodils in the back yard had not yet flowered, and there were few leaves on the trees; nothing yet to cover the dead brown of winter. She stared out the bathroom window, understanding her mistake: she had not known yesterday that the Catskill Mountains in early April were a bleak land of thawing mud.

She could hear Mark downstairs, a loud, reassuring chaos to his movements, and could smell bacon and maple syrup. He probably knew she was awake now, because the bathtub tap sounded like a small explosion when it was first turned on.

She sprinkled herself with some of the lavender talc she found underneath the sink and took a sedative, tasting lavender chalk on her fingers. She did not particularly feel like getting dressed yet, but the cottage was so dark and dusty, she did not like to wander around in it wearing only her nightgown. So she pulled a flannel shirt from her overnight bag and climbed back into her blue jeans.

She found Mark in the kitchen, dribbling pancake batter into a cast-iron pan. A mound of flabby bacon was

draining on a paper towel. Unshaven, his hair an un-
washed, tussled mop, he reminded her of the young
drug addicts who sleep on stoops in the Bowery.

"Morning," she said, giving him a halfhearted smile.

Mark turned to her, hugging her and asking how she
felt.

"I'm okay," she mumbled. "Have you been awake
long?"

"About two hours. I got up around eight-thirty.
How did you sleep?"

"I slept fine. These drugs are an amazing thing."

"Hungry?"

"It looks delicious, but no, I'm not very hungry."

"Not at all?" Mark asked, hurt.

"Okay, I'll have a little," she said to make him
happy. She picked up the phone she saw on the wall by
the refrigerator, and despite the fact she knew there
would be no dial tone, put the receiver to her ear. "Don't
you feel isolated without a phone?" she asked, replacing
the receiver.

"Isn't that the point? Isn't that why we're here?"

She shrugged. "I guess I'm more dependent on the
phone than I thought."

"I don't see what you'd do with a phone right now
even if it was hooked up," he said, a touch of irritation
creeping into his voice.

"I just feel out of touch," she continued easily, not
wanting to quarrel. "Maybe I'd call Christine to see how
she was feeling. Or Kate Hemmick, to see when
Melanie's funeral is."

"Heckler said you shouldn't go to Melanie's funeral."

"I'd still like to know when it is," she said, and then
added, "Come to think of it, Heckler himself would probably be the first person I'd call. For all we know, the police already have caught Penny's and Melanie's killer.
And we can go home."

"I'm sure Heckler would be in touch with us if that were true."

"How?"

"Through the police up here. With a messenger."

"Seems to me a phone would be easier."

Mark flipped the pancakes and then turned to Lisa. "We do not have a working phone," he said, condescending to her by spitting out each syllable. "It is that simple. But if you just can't live without one, I would be happy to drive you to the Dunville Grand Union. They have a pay phone there."

"Why are you getting so bent out of shape about this?"

"I'm not. I just offered to drive you into town, didn't I?"

She started to answer his question directly, but stopped herself. She was too tired and had been through too much to argue with Mark now. If he was going to become a prick suddenly, that would remain his own business. "I'm going down to the dock," she said simply.

"What about breakfast?"

"I've lost my appetite," she told him, grabbing her C.P.O. jacket on her way out the door.

Heckler spent Monday morning in the station house, flipping through the Noble and Braverman homicide photos like baseball cards. It was an exercise in frustration, Heckler knew; it was just one more way he could work to bring his investigation nowhere. When he was through, he had learned absolutely nothing.

Amazingly, there were detectives who envied Heckler, the ones who characterized the Crosby-Slaughter case as a couple of "good murders"—murders that brought out the best in their investigative skills, murders that challenged them as detectives. These were cops who were in the process of fielding "grounders"—routine homicides that demanded more patience than smarts.

Heckler didn't think the envy was justified, and thought to himself that he could use a grounder right now. For four days he had been on this case, and all each day had brought was more questions, not answers. He had a murdered socialite who posed nude because her marriage was shaky, who had planned on buying cocaine for a business meeting. He had a murdered college roommate of that socialite, murdered either because she knew something (but what that something was, was anybody's guess) or simply because she went to Crosby College. He had a murdered coke dealer—low rent, small time, but still highly dead. And last, but certainly not least, was the fact that the two remaining roommates had dropped off the face of the earth: one into the middle of the Catskill Mountains, one God alone knew where.

At ten-thirty he phoned Christine's apartment one last time, and then the Hallmark store in which she worked. Her answering machine was still on at home, and a woman Christine worked with at the card store politely informed Heckler that Christine had not shown up for work that morning. It was "extraordinary," the woman said, completely unlike her. Christine had never before "just not shown up."

More depressed by the news than he had expected to be, Heckler forgot to thank the woman before hanging up. In his mind's eye he saw Christine Yarbrough, her body bloated more than usual by death, wedged into a bathroom stall in an airport restroom. He had no idea why he envisioned her in a bathroom, and felt guilty: she deserved better than an airport toilet. But where else could one hide a body that big at the Delta Terminal, the last place anyone had seen her?

He wandered slowly across the precinct to a dispatcher, his head unhappily fuzzy, to fill out the forms that would make Christine Yarbrough a missing person. It had now been twenty-four hours, and she was officially gone. He then called the airport security people to request a search of the bathrooms and bars and parking lots scattered throughout La Guardia.

He wondered what he could have done differently that might have kept Christine alive. Should he have made her leave New York Saturday night, literally forced her on to a plane? Should he have found her a private bodyguard, regardless of the cost? Or should he have insisted that the NYPD find a way to protect the woman, look out for her as they might a key witness for the prosecution?

He was reminded of his first meeting with Christine, not quite a week earlier, when she had suggested to him that she was responsible for Penny's death. Why? Because she hadn't accompanied Penny to Harris Cohn's apartment. He remembered telling her then that she had had nothing to do with Penny's death, and he had meant it. The fact remained, Penny Noble would probably have died regardless of whether Christine went with her that night to Greenwich Village. And the same was probably true now for himself, Heckler thought: Christine Yarbrough would in all likelihood be dead even if he had tried to get her on a plane on Saturday or had found her a bodyguard. That's just how life was. Who, after all, expects to be massacred when they wander into a McDonald's for a Muppet Baby Happy Meal? What mother would ever let her daughter near a shopping mall if she knew a psychotic ex-Marine planned on opening fire on the Orange Julius concession stand? Would we ever look up in wonder at the skyscrapers around us if we thought for one moment there was a solitary crazy atop one tower with an automatic?

He felt bad for Christine, her death saddened him more than it angered him . . . but he had to move on. He had to concern himself with Lisa Stone, because clearly she was next. Fortunately, she—and Mark—were out of town.

Mark. The idea that Lisa was alone with Mark Scher

began to gnaw at Heckler, to concern him for reasons he couldn't quite explain. He knew there were no grounds for being alarmed, and yet he was. As he focused on the missing persons report before him, it clicked: Mark Scher had driven Christine to the airport. He was the last person to have seen her alive.

Lisa sat at the edge of Mark's dock, leaning against a railing, and wondered when something would sink in and she would become hysterical. It was only a matter of time, it had to be. She should be petrified, horrified, afraid to move. Afraid to crawl out from under her covers, afraid to wander around the house, afraid to sit on the dock. But she wasn't. She was unhappy, she was sure of that, and she might go so far as to classify herself as nervous, or anxious, or uneasy. But terrified? No, she definitely wasn't terrified. She had been much more scared in Gordon's car Friday night, or in Mark's apartment Saturday night. And the fear she had felt at even those moments was nothing compared to the honest-to-God, this-is-it, that's-all-she-wrote horror she had experienced when Melanie was killed. *That* was terrified.

Scanning the lake, she tried counting the number of cottages around it. She could only see three other houses, but judging by the number of docks, there were a good many more. Like Mark's home, most of the cottages were nestled in the woods, thirty to fifty yards away from the water. She guessed there were probably thirty-five other houses on Chippewa Lake.

She did not believe, however, that there were any other people on Chippewa Lake. Not on a cold, cloudy Monday in early April. Chippewa Lake was a summer lake, a man-made summer camp for families. She imagined that the place was rather charming in the proper season—fireworks on the Fourth of July, teenage girls sunning themselves on the docks, overweight little boys on tremendous rafts, floating—but in April, it was a lonely little pond. Deserted, empty, unhappy. The place felt just plain murky to Lisa.

It was too quiet, for one thing. There was something eerie about a Chippewa silence. Usually quiet appealed to Lisa. In New Hampshire, for instance, the quiet had always been a welcome respite from Manhattan—from the unearthly sobs of garbage trucks in reverse, the ceaseless howling of car alarms, the angry, growling acceleration of the avenue buses. But the quiet wasn't appealing now, it was actually somewhat disturbing. It unnaturally magnified for her every sound she made. The broken twig snapped in her fingers like a delivery van backfiring. The dock swayed beneath her with a heavy-handed creak reminiscent of the subway braking to a stop at Fourteenth Street. Her breathing seemed to her the loudest noise on the lake, louder even than the sound the water made when it lapped periodically against the small wharf. It was as if she were the only one in the Catskill Mountains making any noise, as if she and an entire national forest were conspiring together to signal to Leslie Nichols or Ed Simmonds or Gordon Noble exactly where she was, exactly where to find her. She suddenly had the sense of being watched she had experienced for much of Thursday and Friday, but when she looked back at the house, she didn't see Mark in any of the windows.

It crossed her mind that Mark should have come down to the dock by now to apologize. She had been sure he would eat his chewy pancakes, stewing, and then realize he was wrong and stroll down to the water to say he was sorry. Because clearly in this case he was wrong, and the attorney in him eventually would come to that conclusion. That was one of the things she respected in Mark: his ability to see things from her perspective, and when something was his fault, to say so. Wasn't that exactly what had happened Friday morning?

Glancing again around the lake she saw no signs of

life at all. But she was positive she was being watched, she could feel it. She bit her lip and rose, cautiously, using her good arm to hold on to the railing. As she stood, Chippewa Lake rolled below her, tossing the dock and making her stumble slightly. She turned back toward the water, the surface of it a flat black slab, a slab without sheen or luster or glaze, and wondered if anything lived in it. Perhaps some game warden stocked the water with trout in May, but now—did anything live in that unfriendly, forbidding lake now?

As if in answer to her question the water rose again, jarring the dock and making Lisa grab the handrail for balance.

"Only an idiot would be on Chippewa Lake right now," Dunville police captain Stub Waits told Heckler. "As far as I know, most of those places aren't winterized."

"I'm telling you, a man named Mark Scher and a woman named Lisa Stone went there yesterday," Heckler calmly insisted. "They blew this clambake—"

"They blew this what?"

"They left New York City."

"God bless 'em, I would too."

"They left New York City and went to Mark Scher's house on Chippewa Lake."

"Okay, so two New York City idiots are freezing their fannies off on Chippewa Lake. What do you want from my young life?" There was no hostility in Waits's remark, just disbelief: there was no end, it probably seemed to Waits, to the stupidity of city folk. Heckler thought the man might burst into laughter at any moment.

"Well, I was hoping you could spin by the Scher house. I think there could be some trouble up there."

"What kind of trouble?"

"Have you been following the Noble and Braverman homicide investigations?"

"If I followed every homicide in your town, I wouldn't have time to button my fly in the morning."

"'Crosby-Slaughter,'" Heckler added.

"I have seen that in a couple papers, I have."

Heckler envisioned Waits as two tremendous globes cut in half by a holster—squeezed by that holster so that a roll of flab sat in his pants like a bowl of cooked pasta below his belt. "How much do you know about it?" Heckler asked.

"I know I'm glad my little girl never roomed with those people."

"It's not nearly as bad as the newspapers make it sound."

"I'm sure it isn't, Detective. But I got a daughter and I got a niece. Joyce, my daughter, graduated last June from the state university over at Binghamton, and now teaches second graders how to read in Albany. She's dating a boy she met at school, an insurance salesman. My niece, Cathy, is a nurse at the county hospital. She's married, and she has the cutest baby girl you've ever seen. Smart too. Only eleven months old, but you say 'book,' and she'll go bring you a book to read to her. Darnedest thing you've ever seen."

"I'll bet it is," Heckler said agreeably, consciously ignoring Waits's hidden message. He was becoming impatient and wanted to move on.

"And now you're telling me I got these 'Crosby-Slaughter' people in my backyard."

"There were four roommates at college, Captain. Two are definitely dead. Penelope Noble and Melanie Braverman. A third is missing and in all likelihood dead. Christine Yarbrough. The fourth, Lisa Stone, is right now in a house on Chippewa Lake."

"And you want me to drive by and say hello."

"Yes."

"What the hell for?"

"Because I'm beginning to believe the man she's

with—Scher—may have murdered her three room-mates."

"Why?"

Heckler took a breath and paused, leaning back in his chair. "I'm not clear yet on his motive. But I think he's up to something with Gordon Noble—Penelope's husband. Something to do with drugs, maybe. Or it could be something these women haven't told me. I think they had a lot of secrets, Captain," Heckler said, playing up to Waits.

"Do you have any evidence that suggests this Scher character is your man?"

"Yesterday morning, he insisted on driving Christine Yarbrough to La Guardia Airport. She never made it. Yesterday afternoon, he was supposed to take Lisa Stone to New Hampshire, to her family's home in the White Mountains. Somewhere in Connecticut, he changed his mind and brought her to Chippewa Lake instead, to his own summer house."

"What's this man's involvement with Lisa Stone?"

"He's her boyfriend. But he knew all of Lisa's room-mates, and he's a friend of the widower of the first woman killed—Gordon Noble."

"Can I tell you something, Detective?"

"Sure."

"You've got yourself a pile of circumstantials. You've got no probable cause—"

"I realize that," Heckler said, cutting Waits off. "I understand that. All I want you to do is send an officer up to the house to say hello, so that Scher—if he is involved—knows I know exactly where he is."

"Yup, that'll stop him all right," Waits said sarcastically.

"I'm after time, Captain!" Heckler snapped. "As soon as I get off the phone with you, I plan on driving there myself to talk to the man. But Chippewa Lake is a couple of hours from here, and I don't know if I have a couple hours!"

"It's two hours, Detective. *Dos*. If you're that uptight about this, I suggest you get in your car right now instead of jawing with me, and come on up. I'd be happier than a pig in shit to give you directions."

"Does that mean you won't send a car by the house?"

"There are no grounds for that, Detective! You've got no evidence."

"I've got my hunches, Waits! I've been in this business a long time, I'm no rookie! And I'm not asking a hell of a lot of your people."

After a brief moment of silence Waits said, "Tell you what I'll do. I'll send a car around the lake, right past Scher's house. If the patrolmen see any trouble, they'll stop by. How's that?"

"I guess that will have to do."

"I guess it will," Waits said, just a hint of condescension in his voice.

Lisa sat in the Adirondack chair beside the dock, slightly more comfortable on the shore than she had been as a focal point twenty-five feet into the middle of the lake. She was further calmed by the sight of the patrol car that drove slowly past the house around 11:15. It struck Lisa as Heckler's way of saying hello, his way of letting her know that everything was okay. She wasn't sure, but she thought one of the two officers saw her and waved.

Yet even on shore, even with a police car passing by, she felt uneasy. Every time she closed her eyes and tried to relax, she saw hands closing tightly around her neck. Sometimes they were Gordon Noble's large, pale, manicured hands, and sometimes they were Leslie Nichols's—darker and hairier than Gordon's, but just as groomed—but always they grabbed her from behind, squeezing her throat until she choked. Immediately she would open her eyes, half-expecting to realize it was only her imagination just in time for a real hand to reach up from below the Adirondack chair, grab her ankle, and pull her . . .

Pull her where?

It didn't make sense to confuse real murders with the supernatural, and yet she did. The forest was filled with demons, the lake was filled with ghosts. Everywhere she went, death went with her, she decided morosely.

Periodically she looked back at the house, her grounding in reality. After all, Mark was inside. And each time she glanced at the cottage, she expected to see Mark on his way down the back steps to apologize. She had been down by the water for almost forty-five minutes, and still he hadn't materialized. He was never this stubborn, this just wasn't like him.

But then, she thought, it wasn't like her either. She too was being stubborn, sitting alone by the lake with a forty-degree chill in the air.

It was time to make peace. If Mark couldn't say he was sorry right now, she would say it for him. For them. The last thing she needed right now was to squabble with Mark.

Halfway up the hill, she paused. Could the house get any quieter? Suddenly it looked and felt to Lisa as if the house were completely empty, as if Mark had left, or had been swallowed whole by it. She envisioned two of the upstairs windows as eyes, big, tired, drooping eyes, eyes made sad by the dingy sheers pulled tight by dingy lace. The mouth, the mouth that had eaten Mark, was the sagging porch with slashed screens.

She resumed walking, forcing herself back to reality. Mark had to be inside. He was probably reading on the couch. Perhaps he had even dozed off on the couch. . . .

She had, suddenly, a vision of a lump. A lump of beige, a lump of thick black hair, a lump of red. Sitting on the couch in the living room, his legs tucked under his chin, was Mark Scher. At least it had been Mark Scher, judging by the shirt and hair. It was hard to tell from the face, because all that remained of what were once impressively high cheekbones and piercing brown eyes was a scabby, concave, cherry mask. It was as if his face had been smashed with a sledge hammer. There were no eyes, no discernible nose, no chin extending out over his chest. Just a series of dry, scabby leaves, once skin and muscle and bone, dripping almost gracefully down into his neck . . .

Maybe I am hysterical, Lisa thought. She had wondered why she hadn't become hysterical sooner, when perhaps she had been all along. She didn't imagine that a stable individual envisioned her boyfriend's skull crushed in like a truffle.

She opened the back door to the house very slowly, her eyes scanning the hallway and kitchen. The hall closet was half-open, as she had left it, and the maple spread and pancake batter were still sitting on the kitchen counter beside the stove. The skillet was in the sink, as were the plates. She hung up the C.P.O. jacket and shut the closet, and then cut through the kitchen to the dining room.

"Mark?" she called, hearing no sound in the dining room. "Mark?"

She saw his coffee mug on the dining-room table where he had sat, a dark brown ring forming around it on the white place mat. She passed through the dining room into the living room, glancing behind her and before her as she recrossed the hallway. Mark was not in the living room either.

"Mark?" she called again, becoming afraid. "Where are you?"

When there was no response, she became completely still. She could feel the veins in her left arm throbbing against her stitches, and could hear her heart pounding furiously in her head. It seemed so loud to her that whoever was in the house with her must have heard it too. Whoever. Light-headed with fear, she nevertheless knew she had to get out. She could leave through the front door, but that would mean walking the length of the hallway, past both the stairway to the second floor and the door to the basement. She could rush out the back door, but she would then have to pass through the dining room and the kitchen. The safest, most direct way out might simply be through the picture window in the living room. She was not positive she could raise it with one hand, but she decided to try. She stepped backward to the window as silently as possible, both to hear any other movement in the house and to minimize any chance that she herself would be heard.

When she reached the window, she turned slightly so she could raise it with her right arm, yet still see the entrance to the living room. There would be no way to open the window quietly: if she raised it slowly, it would groan like the dock; if she threw it open quickly, it would rattle in its tracks like thunder. She opted for speed and thunder, reached for the bottom of the frame, and hoisted it open in one movement.

The sound echoed briefly, but when it stopped the house became completely still. Using her good arm for support, she swung first her left leg and then her right over the sill, so that within seconds she was outside. Back outside, she thought, relieved. Now she had to get to the police, because clearly something had happened to Mark.

She ran down the walk to the driveway, hoping the keys were in the Catalina, and planned to leave. She would get out, she would get out now. She would drive away as fast as possible.

She opened the door and peered in at the ignition. The key wasn't there, nor was it anywhere on the dashboard or on the front seat. It must still be on the kitchen counter, where Mark had thrown it the night before. There was no way Lisa would go back into the house after it, however, not now. She would simply run away on foot, into the woods, so without bothering to slam the car door she turned to flee. But she did not run far, because when she turned around, a large figure in a blue and orange New York Mets ski mask rushed at her from the woods. Vaguely aware in some distant part of her brain that it was over, that she had lost, she nevertheless lashed out with all the energy she had left. She tried to kick Ski Mask in the crotch, while pounding her fist into his head. The kick didn't stun him, but it must have hurt him, because he nearly doubled over before he grabbed her right arm and threw her against the car. In the moment before her head smacked against the open door, the moment before she crumpled into an unconscious heap on the rocky driveway, she wondered whatever happened to the good old days when ski masks were only used for skiing.

30

"Stupid Little Priss"

Heckler was well past the first highway billboards for the Concord, the Nevele, and Grossinger's—the Catskills' premier resorts—when he saw the exit he was looking for. On the off ramp he noticed it was also the exit for the Catskills' largest designer shoe and cowboy boot outlet. He was just south of Monticello.

Coasting to a stop for the first time since leaving Manhattan, he looked at the directions Waits had given him and decided he was about fifteen minutes from Chippewa Lake. For a moment his mind wandered at the stop sign, and he realized he had never bothered to cancel his afternoon meeting at Dayton-Patterson. If he were right about Mark Scher, however, it probably didn't matter.

He wondered how he could have misread the boyfriend. It had never crossed his mind that Mark was somehow involved in these murders—with squash buddy Gordon Noble, perhaps—and yet the signals must have been there. At least they always had been in the past: an unreasonable intensity, unusual outbursts, jitters, paranoia, melancholy. But Mark Scher? The guy seemed too damn casual to kill anyone.

Lisa woke up on the living-room couch with a wonderful sense of slow motion. Her arm was throbbing, but she was warm and comfortable and groggy. She was covered with what she thought was a reading blanket, but was in actuality a large plaid shawl.

She came to her senses quickly, however, when she saw Christine kneeling on the floor beside her. She knew—knew positively, knew with an instinctive, lacerating pang that cut worse than the knife Friday night— that Christine Yarbrough had murdered her own best friends.

"Oh God, Christine," she said, her voice little more than a hoarse whisper, "Oh God, why?"

Christine smiled, putting her hands into the front pocket of her baggy sweatshirt. "Oh, man, Lis, if you only knew. This whole thing is so far outta control. I never meant to hurt anyone, and all of the sudden the whole world is comin' up dead on me."

"How did you find us? Me?"

"Lover boy Scher told me 'bout this bit o' paradise on the way to the airport. He was already gettin' cold feet 'bout Sugar Hill," Christine answered, her accent much thicker than usual.

"Is Mark . . . is Mark all right?"

"Yeah, Mark's fine. He's out like a rock, but he's fine."

"What do you want from me?" Lisa asked, her voice still barely audible.

Christine sat back on her haunches and then reached inside her sweatshirt, pulling out the New York Mets ski mask. "I've never looked good in blue, have I? Blue has always been your color," she said slowly, before tossing the ski mask at her old roommate. Reflexively Lisa squirmed, trying to duck the mask as if it were a newly dead animal. "Two bucks from a street kid," she added.

Carefully Lisa sat up on the couch, instinctively pulling her legs before her chest in defense. She started again to ask why, but stifled the question in her throat, deciding that the worst possible thing she could do now would be to antagonize Christine. "Blue never looks good on brunettes," she said softly, hoping her comment didn't sound as absurd to Christine as it did to herself. She wished she had kept her eyes closed and feigned sleep until help arrived.

"You're such a fucking account executive, Lis. Always the diplomat, even at the bitter end."

The words demolished Lisa's faint hope that Christine didn't plan on killing her. "Is this the bitter end?" she asked, almost rhetorically.

"Yeah, I'm afraid it has to be. I couldn't bring myself to wrap things up with you outside, Lis, but I was jus' postponin' the inevitable, I guess. I must admit, I didn't really mind killin' Melanie, and I never meant to kill Penny, but you—I wish it had never come to this for you, Lis."

"I don't understand. What do you mean you never meant to kill Penny?"

"Just what it sounds like. I never woulda murdered that good woman if I hadn't seen with my own eyes all that cash on the coffee table—"

"You killed Penny for money?" Lisa asked, astonished. Immediately she regretted the outburst, afraid that she had angered Christine.

"No, that's not it at all," Christine said petulantly. "I mean, yes, I did kill Penny. God, that sounds funny to say. But the thing is, I didn't go there planning to kill her. Hell, I didn't even go to that Harris guy's place with her planning to steal anything.

"It was all sorta spontaneous. I knew Penny was

goin' there to get those artsy-fartsy pictures taken to juice up Gordon, and I knew she was goin' there to buy about a ton of cocaine for that dumb-ass sales meeting. But I didn't put two and two together till she started flashin' the cash."

"I'm not sure I see the connection," Lisa said. She began scanning the room to see if there was anything she could use as a weapon. Even if she found a weapon, however, she wondered if she were actually capable of hurting Christine, her old friend and roommate.

"I believe the word is blackmail, Lisa. Maybe extortion. Suddenly, only two feet to my right, Penny is dealing out ten, twenty, thirty grand. Maybe that's not a lot of bread to you, but it is to me. It's more money than I net in a whole year, and it's right there on the coffee table! Not two feet from me, Lis! And on the other side of me is my ticket to all that money. A drug deal. And a roll of film on which Penny Noble—of course I mean the Penny Noble of Park Avenue and Dayton-Patterson—is posing half-naked, and three-quarters naked, and completely bare bottom naked some of the time.

"This, I said to myself, is fate. Kismet. This money is mine for the takin'. I didn't want to hurt Penny, understand that, but my God, what was thirty grand to her? It was squat to her, that's what it was. But it was the world to me. It could have been for me the start of a whole new life. So I made them my offer: they give me the money, and I don't show the negatives or the pictures to anyone, and I don't tell anyone about their little drug deal.

"And you know what they did? What he did? That creepy guy Cohn pulled a gun on me!"

The best weapon was probably the wrought iron poker, Lisa decided. Unfortunately, Christine was sitting directly between her and the fireplace.

"From that second on, the room just went berserk," Christine continued. "Penny tried to get him to put the gun down, and managed to distract him. So I jumped him, and yanked his gun away. After that, there's no way I can give you a blow-by-blow, because it all happened so fast. I'm shootin' and Harris is runnin' and Penny is screamin'. It was just chaos. And when the smoke cleared . . . well, I don't have to tell you what happened when the smoke cleared."

Lisa thought Christine sounded incredulous. "It was that easy?" she asked.

Christine shook her head yes. "Yeah, Lis, murder—the act itself—is easy. Especially after you've done it once. Especially if the first one just sorta happens. Like with Penny. Hell, I was half-defendin' myself when I shot Harris Cohn.

"It's after the murder that life gets hard. You wonder: did I leave the place with blood on me? Where did I leave fingerprints? Did I remember my wallet? You relive it over and over, and you always recall something you did wrong. Something that's gonna get you snagged."

Lisa noticed for the first time that Christine was wearing a watch, but she could not see the time because the cuff of her sweatshirt covered most of her wrist. She wondered what the odds were of a Dunville police officer actually knocking on the door to say hello, and decided they were probably pretty slim. Still, Heckler didn't like to leave a lot of things to chance. The best thing she could do, she concluded, would be to keep Christine talking as long as possible. "How did Melanie find out you . . . you did it?" she asked.

"That's what I mean," Christine said, spreading wide her arms. "I left Harris Cohn's Wednesday night and rinsed out all my clothes, took about a two-hour shower. But still I missed something. And you know what that was?"

"No."

"The strap to my goddamn purse! Can you believe it? The strap to my purse! There was a splotch of blood on it, and Melanie picked up on it the second she saw it."

"So you killed her?"

"You panic after a murder, Lisa. That's what I mean about it bein' so tough. You panic, you go a little berserk. You don't think straight. So yes, I killed Melanie. 'Course, I didn't mind killin' Melanie quite so much. You know Mel and me didn't always see eye to eye exactly.

"Still. Killin' Mel started that cycle of worrying all over again. Who saw me? What did they see? What did I leave at the scene of the crime? You live with all these fears, you're convinced everyone knows you did it. The *Post*. The police. I was convinced that Heckler would pick me up any minute, especially when he was jabberin' on about pros and amateurs."

"No one tried to break into Mark's apartment Saturday night, did they?" Lisa said. "You made that up, didn't you?"

"I panicked. You really had me nervous, Lis. I thought I had to get you to stop nosin' around, and there was only one sure way to do that . . . If I hadn't made such a goddamn racket with the door when I was gettin' Mark's knife, you would never have seen Sunday morning."

"What do you plan to do now?"

Ignoring her, Christine rose and wandered back to the fireplace, resting her arm against the mantle like a diplomat in a brandy ad. "Bet you didn't think I had it in me, did you?"

"I don't know," Lisa answered, stalling while she concocted a response. "I don't know. I guess I've always thought you could do anything you wanted, once you put your mind to it."

"Think so? Then tell me: if I put my mind to it, think I could lose fifty pounds?"

"Yes, of course."

"You're lyin', Lis, I can always tell. You know as well as I do I could do no such thing. You know I couldn't lose twenty pounds if I had to, much less fifty. That's why I can't believe you're not surprised I've managed to shrink the size of our reunion class a wee bit. Don't kid me, Lis:

it never crossed your mind for one second this weekend that I killed Penny or Melanie."

"No," she said, "but only because I thought the killer was a man."

"You're such a sexist, Lis! Four fucking years at Crosby, and you still think all murderers are men. You little priss, you," Christine said, before abruptly running her arm over the mantle and smashing on to the floor the two porcelain hunting dogs that had rested on it. "You stupid, stupid little priss!"

Lisa flinched, surprised by Christine's sudden outburst. Perhaps she couldn't simply wait for help to arrive; perhaps she would have to try and beat Christine to the fireplace poker after all, and . . . Good God, she thought, defend herself against one of her oldest, closest friends with a ten-pound club of wrought iron. She wasn't sure she had it in her.

"You and Penny and Melanie. You were all such little prisses," Christine continued, her tone clipped and angry. She pushed some of the splintered pieces of china into the fireplace with her foot. "All pretty, all popular . . . and you were all so close. You and Penny were close, and you and Melanie were close, but me? I was never close to any of you. You wouldn't let me. You always treated me as the pathetic one, the one who stayed home alone on Saturday nights watching television. I was the one with the weight problem, I was the one who needed help. I was the outsider."

Lisa knew she couldn't overpower Christine with a sudden charge, especially with her left arm a mass of unweaving stitches. Christine, however, was on the far side of the mantle from the poker, virtually as far away from the weapon as she herself was.

"Christine, I also felt left out sometimes," Lisa told her, hoping to calm Christine to the point where she could beat the larger woman to the poker. "And I'm sure Penny and Melanie did too. We all had our secrets. We all had our own separate lives."

"And mine always seemed to count for less than yours. Until now."

"Will killing me make you happy?" Lisa asked quickly. "Killing Penny and Melanie sure didn't—"

"That's not the point!" Christine yelled, cutting her off. She grabbed the poker from its bronze stand, and as if it were a riding crop snapped it against the hurricane lamp beside the fireplace, reducing the lamp to a dozen jagged pieces of glass. "If I wanted to kill you, don't you think I would have by now?" she asked.

"Then don't do it—"

"Goddamn, I've wasted too much time as it is," Christine hissed, starting toward Lisa. She gripped the poker with both hands as if it were a baseball bat, and raised it above her head. "You're no better than they were, so you can just go 'n take your secrets and separate lives bullshit to your grave!"

Instinctively Lisa threw her arms before her face and started to rise. For one brief second she could see the shock and anger in Christine's eyes that she had stood to face her, to challenge her, but that second didn't last long because at the moment she stood the room seemed to explode. There was one thunderous, reverberating bang, followed instantly by a storm of flying glass. Convinced that a plane was crashing into the house, she ducked, closing her eyes reflexively and falling back on the couch. When only the echo remained a moment later, when she heard the last bits of broken glass tinkle to the floor, she looked up, half-expecting to see the tip of a small jet in the room.

Instead she saw only broken glass from the picture window scattered across the room, coating everything like a layer of sun-speckled dew. Including Christine, whose body had wound up about five feet from her, blown smack into the wall adjacent the couch. It was a crumpled mass, the left side of her face crosshatched by bleeding glass cuts. A gurgling red fountain had opened where the back of her head used to be.

Lisa whirled away from Christine toward the hole in the opposite wall that was once the picture window. There, dwarfed both by a Catskill foothill and the rows of pine trees, was Richard Heckler, the detective with the black bristle haircut.

VII

Tuesday

31

Lisa's Other Dream

Richard Heckler tossed the new bag of kitty litter off to the side and began to sweep the old cat sand off the floor. It never ceased to amaze him that a cat as compulsively clean as Cubber could make such a mess.

He wondered how Lisa Stone was feeling, assuming she was capable of feeling anything at all. She had not seemed angry at Mark for taking her to the Catskills, and then lying to her about reaching Heckler with his decision ("I didn't want to upset her any more than she already was," he had explained), and that in itself struck Heckler as a good sign. She would get better. Eventually.

When he was through sweeping, he carefully emptied the sand box into a fully opened paper grocery bag, then sponged out the bottom of the plastic tub. Cubber watched him eagerly, practically drooling at the idea of a fresh sand box.

When it was dry, Heckler reached for the Tuesday *New York Post*, the one with Christine Yarbrough on the front page, and placed it flat on the bottom of the litter box.

"Have a ball, little one," he said to the boneless cat. "Have a ball."

Lisa Stone slept curled in a ball, her knees tucked in near her chest. When she rolled over, she knocked to the floor the newspaper she had been reading, the Tuesday *Post* with Christine Yarbrough on the front page.

She dreamt she had written an article about all of her roommates, an article as much about Melanie Braverman and Christine Yarbrough as it was about Penny Noble. In this article, none of the women was dead. They were alive and they were thriving, so much so that the story read almost like the class notes from the college's alumnae quarterly. Penny and Gordon Noble, now new parents, were moving out of Manhattan. Melanie Braverman was getting married, but even more noteworthy was the news that she was letting her hair grow out to its natural color. And Christine Yarbrough, who had lost close to sixty pounds, was returning to law school.

When Lisa woke up she was smiling, and she didn't stop smiling until she saw the ash-colored smudges on the bedspread. She knew immediately those were newspaper smudges, and recalled with a pang the fact that her roommates all were dead. Her eyes began to tear: although she could feel Mark beside her in bed, she had never in her life felt more lonely.

About the Author

CHRISTOPHER A. BOHJALIAN's work has appeared in *Cosmopolitan* and other magazines. He is also a columnist for the *Burlington Free Press*. A graduate of Amherst College, he lives now in a small Vermont village with his wife, four cats, and whatever "mousers" appear in their barn. *A Killing in the Real World* is his first novel, and he is currently working on a second.